# AFRICAN WRITERS SERIES

P9-AFJ-228

AFRICAN WRITERS SERIES
Editorial Adviser   Chinua Achebe

# Bound to Violence

# BOUND TO VIOLENCE

## Yambo Ouologuem

Translated from the French by Ralph Manheim

**HEINEMANN**
LONDON · IBADAN · NAIROBI

Heinemann Educational Books Ltd
22 Bedford Square, London WC1B 3HH
P.M.B. 5205 Ibadan · P.O. BOX 45314 Nairobi

EDINBURGH MELBOURNE AUCKLAND
HONG KONG SINGAPORE KUALA LUMPUR
NEW DELHI KINGSTON

Heinemann Educational Books Inc.
70 Court Street, Portsmouth, New Hampshire 03801, USA

ISBN 0 435 90099 4

Acknowledgement

The Publishers acknowledge the use of certain
passages on pages 54–56 from *It's a Battlefield* by
Graham Greene

Printed in Great Britain by
Richard Clay (The Chaucer Press) Ltd,
Bungay, Suffolk

*To the humble companion of bad days and worse.*

ONE

# The Legend of the Saifs

Our eyes drink the brightness of the sun and, overcome, marvel at their tears. *Mashallah! wa bismillah!* . . . To recount the bloody adventure of the niggertrash—shame to the worthless paupers!—there would be no need to go back beyond the present century; but the true history of the Blacks begins much earlier, with the Saifs,* in the year 1202 of our era, in the African Empire of Nakem south of Fezzan, long after the conquests of Okba ben Nafi al-Fitri.

The fame of that Empire spread to Morocco, the Sudan, Egypt, Abyssinia, and to the holy and noble city of Mecca; it was known to the English, the Dutch, the French, the Spaniards, and, it goes without saying, the Portuguese. An account of its splendor would be empty folklore.

What is more interesting, when the elders, notables, and griots,† peering wide-eyed into the bitter deserts, speak of that

---

* Pronounced Sah-yeefs.
† Griot: a troubadour, member of a hereditary caste whose function it is to celebrate the great events of history and to uphold the God-given traditions. Y.O.

3

Empire, is the desperate flight, before God's implacable "blessing," of its population, baptized in torture, hunted as far as the Rande, dispersed along the barren mountains of Goro Foto Zinko, strewn about the islands of the Yame River for a distance of more than fifteen hundred miles downstream from Ziuko, occupying remote frontiers on the Atlantic coast, scattered over the savannas bordering on Equatorial Africa, forming groups of varying sizes, separated from one another by all manner of tribes—Radingues, Fulani, Gonda, nomadic Berbers, Ngodo—torn by internecine rivalries and warring with one another for the imperial power with a violence equaled only by the dread it called forth.

By way of reprisal the Saifs—with cries of "For the glory of the world!"—stained their assegais in crime and tribal exactions.

In that age of feudalism, large communities of slaves celebrated the justice of their overlords by forced labor and by looking on inert as multitudes of their brothers, smeared with the blood of butchered children and of disemboweled expectant mothers, were immured alive. . . . That is what happened at Tillabéri-Bentia, at Granta, at Grosso, at Gagol-Gosso, and in many places mentioned in the *Tarik al-Fetach* and the *Tarik al-Sudan* of the Arab historians.

Afterwards wild supplication was heard from the village square to the dark thickets where the hyenas sleep. Then pious silence, and the griot Kutuli of cherished memory ends his tale as follows: "Not far from the bodies of the countless slaughtered children, seventeen fetuses were counted, expelled from the gaping entrails of mothers in death agony. Under the eyes of all, those women had been raped by their husbands, who then, overpowered by shame, had killed themselves. And they could not shrink back from this suicide, not even to save the life of one of their brothers, a helpless witness to the scene, whose expression, marked by the incredulity of despair, was judged—*Al'allah!*—to be "unduly tearful" or "less terrified than usual."

The village chief, his lips parted in silent, breathless resignation, drew the conclusion that human life was vain. Though he was shaken to the point of madness, it was nevertheless his duty to discourage rebellious minds by displaying, on a fan plaited from reeds, the ear lobes of other rebellious men from the neighboring village, whose bodies had been converted into ashes and scattered over the river. . . . The malefic spirits of those beggars, so it was said, contaminated the waters for at least three years, obliging the few able-bodied men in the village to dig wells at a safe distance, which were guarded at night against the spirits of evil: upon them the mercies of the Most-High and the choicest of blessings.

But there is nothing unusual in this story: many others relate how terror enslaved the populations and stifled every attempt at rebellion throughout the Empire. For two more centuries the heart of Nakem bore such humiliations and ignominies with patience; the Crown forced men to swallow life as a boa swallows a stinking antelope, and rolled from one inglorious dynasty and sibylline genealogy to another, falling lower with each new act of vileness. . . . Against this background of horror the destiny of Saif Isaac al-Heit stands out most illustriously; rising far above the common lot, it endowed the legend of the Saifs with the splendor in which the dreamers of African unity sun themselves to this day.

To picture that renaissance of the Nakem Empire through the person of Saif, one must have heard the dismal litany of the imperial dictatorships of those days from the mouths of the elders. It came to pass that one day in the year 1420 Saif Moshe Gabbai of Honain—after hearing the words of a soothsayer who predicted that he would be overthrown by a child to be born during the coming year in Tillabéri-Bentia, capital of the Nakem Empire—ceased to ignore the strange cravings of pregnant women. He consigned all newborn babes to the red death and lined up their shrunken heads along the wall of his antechamber. But one mother, Tiebiramina—how much more fortunate than the rest!—saved her newborn babe under cover of night and fled, followed by her husband and three faithful servants, to Gagol-Gosso, where they settled.

When this son, Isaac al-Heit, had grown to be a strong, brave man, he went off with a troop of warriors.

At this point tradition loses itself in legend, for there are few written accounts and the versions of the elders diverge from those of the griots, which differ in turn from those of the chroniclers.

According to one version, Isaac al-Heit, even before going to war, was a mighty lord whose parents were living out a happy old age among the princes of Rande province. In another version his parents were massacred by one of the punitive expeditions sent out by Saif Moshe Gabbai of Honain; himself pierced by an assegai, he was saved by a Gonda peasant, who cared for him and after many moons healed him. Still others claimed that he joined the troop of warriors because he was drawn to the glory and splendor of warfare.

When the Immortal One makes the sun—diamond of the house of His Power—set, then, along with the tales of the oral tradition, the elders intone the famous epic (the value of which some contest, because they deny Saif's Jewish descent, insisting that he was a plain ordinary nigger) written by Mahmud Meknud Trare, a descendant of griot ancestors and himself a griot of the present-day African Republic of Nakem-Ziuko, which is all that remains of the ancient Nakem Empire:

The Lord—holy is His Name!—showed us the mercy of bringing forth, at the beginning of the black Nakem Empire, one illustrious man, our ancestor the black Jew Abraham al-Heit, born of a black father and of an Oriental Jewess from Kenana (Canaan), descended from Jews of Cyrenaica and Tuat; it is believed that she was carried to Nakem by a secondary migration that followed the itinerary of Cornelius Balbus.

The Most-High did this in His infinite mercy—prayer and peace upon it!—in order to bless the tradition of the Saif dynasty, rooted in the greatness of one man, the most pious and devout Isaac al-Heit, who freed a slave each day. The source of his power was his righteous sacrifice in renouncing his princely possessions to join a passing band of adventurers.

And now behold: The brave and daring Isaac al-Heit knew hunger, thirst, fever, the tumult of battle and the sight of the dying. A hundred times he was given up for dead. Each time, thanks to the favor of the most-just and compassionate Master of the Worlds, he escaped, for his death would have been intolerable to God and to the righteous: *wassalam!*

And behold further: Amidst the mounds of corpses left by the passage of Saif Moshe Gabbai of Honain (God's curse upon him!) the noble ardor of Isaac al-Heit (God refresh his couch) awoke to new life. He drew his sword: the sun and the moon shone on its blade and in it the earth was reflected as in a mirror.

And lastly: the Eternal One blessed Isaac; fugitive slaves, insurgent peasants, the poor and honest, soldiers, adventurers, orphans, all manner of brave men flocked to his banner and formed his army.

It grew. He became famous. And sought-after.

Terrible in battle, he defeated the Berbers, the Moors, and the Tuareg, recognized the Sheikh Mohammed ben Abd-al-Karim al-Meghili, the Sheikh Shamharouk of the race of the Jinn, and the Hassanid Sherif Mulai al-Abbas, Prince of Mecca: God hold them all in His compassion! In Bengazi he fought the enemies of the Imam Abu Bakr ben Omar al-Yemani, in Tripoli he destroyed the usurpers who were plotting to assassinate the Qadi Abd-al-Qahir ben al-Fizan, and one day when he was staying with Beni Tsa'aleb in the province of Algiers, the Sheikh Abd-ar-Rahman al-Tsa'albi brought him the prophecy of Imam Mahmud, Grand Sherif of Mecca: "There will come a new Saif, who will quench the thirst of the men of the Nakem Empire: thou, Isaac al-Heit, art that man, thou art the first, for thou art the water and the salt and the bread, thou art holy and wilt be caliph. After thee, another caliph, descended from the province of Tekrur of the Nakem Empire, will come at the end of the thirteenth century of the Hegira, and the sun will shine on his reign; on both of you God will shower riches, power, and glory, which you will expend on things agreeable to Him."

Some time after this, it is said, the tyrant Saif Moshe Gabbai of Honain—God curse his kingship!—was defeated by Isaac al-Heit and sought safety in flight. The world darkened before his eyes and his face in anger turned as yellow as pepper; by forced marches he arrived at the Yame River, which he descended; in the end he came to southern Sao, where, so it is said, he died of a ruptured gall bladder, leaving the power to the gentle and well-beloved Isaac al-Heit, who took the royal title of Saif, calling himself Saif Isaac al-Heit (God refresh his couch). His countenance was like the lightning and his gown was white; his reign was just and glorious. (God keep his soul.)

Whether truth or invention, the legend of Saif Isaac al-Heit still haunts Black romanticism and the political thinking of the notables in a good many republics. For his memory strikes the popular imagination. Chroniclers draw on the oral tradition to enrich his cult and through him celebrate the glorious era of the first States with their wise philosopher-king, whose history has called not only archaeology, history, and numismatics but also the natural sciences and ethnology to their highest tasks.

Yet it cannot be denied: if the memory of this past—glorious as it was—has survived, it is solely thanks to the Arab historians and to the oral tradition of the Africans, which is as follows:

At his death in 1498 Saif Isaac al-Heit, the mild and just emperor, left three sons: Joshua, who was dedicated to the service of God; Saif al-Haram; and Saif al-Hilal, the youngest; he also left eight daughters and four wives, Ramina, Dogobusseb, Aissina, and Hawa. But seven years before, the Emperor Saif Isaac al-Heit, while mounting his horse during the feast of Tabaski, missed the saddle and tumbled head over heels. Sorely grieved, Saif al-Hilal, the youngest son, ran to his father and helped him to rise, but his elder brother, Saif al-Haram, was moved only to mirth; not only did he burst out laughing but, like the irreverent son that he was, he called the incident to the attention of courtiers and stable hands.

That same night, at the hour when the jackals fill the bush with their howling, the emperor gathered together his whole court, the Assembly of Notables, and the Council of Elders, disinherited his second son, Saif al-Haram, and called down malediction and ruin on all his posterity.

Thus at the death of the just and gentle Saif al-Heit (salvation upon him!), his blessed son Saif al-Hilal mounted the imperial throne, but—great the misfortune!—only for thirteen days. For Saif al-Haram proclaimed that the royal pair must consist of the queen mother and her son; all in one night he married his late father's four wives—including Ramina, his own mother—and seized power, after throwing his younger brother, the legitimate heir to the throne, into a dungeon, bound hand and foot.

There Saif al-Hilal was reduced to satisfying his needs in his clothes and, on his knees, with his hands tied behind his back, to lap up the food that was tossed in through the barely opened trap door. On the twelfth day of Ramadan the worms began to eat him alive and on the twentieth day of the same month he died. . . . A prayer for him.

. . . Then the Emperor Saif al-Haram, the wicked brother and accursed son—God's malediction upon him!—returned from a war against the Fulani escorted by twelve thousand Tukulör slaves to Tillabéri-Bentia, the capital, where the people, crushed beneath the sun, were waiting at the gates. His horse pranced majestically as he saluted the frantic crowd. To his right notables, chiefs of the various provinces, court dignitaries, to his left women, children, and old men, behind him the army flanked by long rows of slaves with shackled ankles. A triumphal homecoming; his victories seemed to have washed away his taint.

Entering the courtyard of his palace in full pomp, he was about to alight from his horse to greet his wives, who were at the same time his stepmothers, when suddenly—such be the fate of those who curse Thee!—his horse shied; in his fall he tore the short trousers of his blue tunic, exposing his nether regions to the crowd in the manner of Adam at his birth.

Stunned, the fanatical crowd bore loud witness to its inborn imbecility, for it saw the incident as a divine omen. . . . Several witnesses declared that someone had deliberately filed the horse's girth to provoke a scandal. Their ears were pulled, their heads were shaved, and crosses were tattooed on the soles of their feet in order that each one of their steps might be an offense to God; the imperial sorcerer threatened to curse their fathers, mothers, ancestors, and descendants; and certain courtiers, who had been denounced, were obliged to confess their falsehood to God, who spoke to them through the mouth of the sorcerer; they were banished to Digal, where horses trampled them and shattered their limbs; with a Tuareg dagger, blessed and turned seven times in their eyes, their ears, their testicles, and then slowly in their navels, they were drained of their seditious blood and finally, by burning, recalled to the most-compassionate Master of the Worlds.

But Saif al-Haram, fearing his father's prophecy, so it seems, and wishing to appease the shades of his dead father and his murdered brother, "abdicated" after a long (diplomatic) illness punctuated (also diplomatically) by brilliant victories over the Gutes, the Jakuks, and the Vantungs. The new "emperor," a Tuareg slave, was merely the toady and bodyguard of Saif al-Haram, who, an impassive figure of lava and laterite, did his best from then on to deprive the nobility of all power. The new emperor's name was Abd al-Hassana; a scheming rogue, gentle even in his cruelty.

On the advice of Saif al-Haram, this toady made a pious pilgrimage to Mecca, whence he returned in a year's time bearing the title "Al Hadj," Pilgrim to the Holy Land. By dispensing the holy water of the city of the Prophet, he believed that he could appease the unruly people, cure the palsied, and restore sight to the blind and faith to infidels: *alif lam.*

It soon became evident that the water of the Holy City won him no friends, did not restore sight to the blind, did not cure the palsied, and—oh sacrilege!—did not even taste good, or so the infidels claimed. . . .

Then, telling the beads of evil, Saif al-Haram and his acolyte

Abd al-Hassana "wrought" miracles. On the twentieth day of May 1503, with the complicity of the divine compassion, a pyre burst into flames of its own accord, and on it eighteen notables, faithful to the memory of the just Saif Isaac al-Heit and of his youngest son, were roasted alive; as they were roasting, eighteen slimy asps escaped from under their garments, slithered over the logs, and, guided by the invisible breath of Satan, vanished into little holes which had miraculously appeared in the sand of the imperial courtyard, where they had been dug the day before. . . .

The ecstatic crowd broke into a long howl, as drawn-out as a lion's roar, and fell to their knees singing a hymn. "A miracle!" they roared.

At the hour of the owl's cry, the pyre was still casting its tongues of flame into the blue air, where rose the chants of the muezzins reciting the suras of the Koran.

Later on, to commemorate the historic date of this miracle which had been followed by others equally bloody, Saif decided, in agreement with Al Hadj Abd al-Hassana, to make an enormous fire on the twentieth of May of each ensuing year; they called it the *fire of the vipers of the supernatural*. A national holiday had been established. A hymn to it.

After the death of the just Saif Isaac al-Heit, however, the accursed son Saif al-Haram and his minister Al Hadj Abd al-Hassana, struck by a stone in the soul they did not possess, spent large sums of money supporting the most influential and discontented families at court: twelve thousand dishes were served them at each meal; they received bribes, pensions, and titles of nobility as pompous as they were meaningless; all the magnificence of a fairy tale: their horses, to the number of 3,260, drank milk in mangers inlaid with gold and ivory. *Allah harmin katamadjo!*

To maintain this ostentation and satisfy his craving for glory and new lands, Saif, thanks to the complicity of the southern chiefs, extended the slave trade, which he blessed like the bloodthirsty hypocrite he was. Amidst the diabolical jubilation of priest and merchant, of family circles and public organs, niggers, who unlike God have arms but no soul, were clubbed, sold, stockpiled, haggled over, adjudicated, flogged, bound and delivered—with attentive, studied, sorrowful contempt—to the Portuguese, the Spaniards, the Arabs (on the east and north coasts), and to the French, Dutch, and English (west coast), and so scattered to the winds.

A hundred million of the damned—so moan the troubadours of Nakem when the evening vomits forth its starry diamonds—were carried away. Bound in bundles of six, shorn of all human dignity, they were flung into the Christian incognito of ships' holds, where no light could reach them. And there was not a single trader of souls who dared, on pain of losing his own, to show his head at the hatches. A single hour in that pestilential hole, in that orgy of fever, starvation, vermin, beriberi, scurvy, suffocation, and misery, would have left no man unscathed. Thirty per cent died en route. And, since charity is a fine thing and hardly human, those amiable slavers were obliged when their cargo was unloaded to pay a fine for every dead slave; slaves who were as sick as a goat in labor were thrown to the sharks. Newborn babes incurred the same fate: they were thrown overboard as surplus. . . . Half naked and utterly bewildered, the niggertrash, young as the new moon, were crowded into open pens and auctioned off. There they lay beneath the eyes of the all-powerful (and just) God, a human tide, a black mass of putrid flesh, a spectacle of ebbing life and nameless suffering.

The heap of slaves writhed, cries and moans were heard, bodies were trampled when the trader cracked his whip to wake up the niggers in the front rows. Those who had come to see the sight kept a respectful distance and watched the priests who were here to proclaim the word of Christ but could only fight down their disgust, hang their heads, and let their rosaries slip through their fingers. . . .

Fascinated by the bodies of the slaves or by their quivering sex organs (it happened time and time again), a young girl whose beauty outmarveled her finery, with the piping voice, the restless eye, the fluttering throat of a guinea hen, would turn to her pink-and-white mother, if not for consolation then at least for a sign of interest or an authoritative opinion on black sexuality. One of the charming replies was: "The Holy Father doesn't approve of *café au lait*. . . ."

Others, less circumspect, like the fiery-eyed English pirate Hawkins, made their profit and were knighted by the hand of a queen, Queen Elizabeth among others, which permitted them to enrich their escutcheons with "a demi-Moor in his proper color, bound with a cord." God save the Queen!

Meanwhile at the court of the Nakem Empire, the unpopular Saif al-Haram, once the restive nobility had been domesticated, incited his minister to stir up "as much trouble as possible" between the backward, untamable, and perpetually warring tribes.

For there were no lengths to which Saif would not go to obtain cattle, land, and other capital goods. Engineered with a more than Machiavellian guile, the raids of the Masai, the Zulus, the Jaga so infuriated the victimized tribes, races, and peoples (so it was ordained from On High) that an entire tribe would tremble with impatience when its chief, hurling his lance in the direction of the "enemy race" (accused of having carried off such and such villagers and sold them into slavery), roared that the time had come for their assegais to drink the accursed enemy blood.

Cruel peoples, whose speech is a kind of croaking, fierce killers, men of the jungle, living in a state of bestiality, mating with the first woman they find, tall in stature and horrible to look upon, hairy men with abnormally long nails, the Zulus, Jaga, and Masai feed on human flesh and go naked, armed with shields, darts, and daggers. Savage in their customs and daily lives, they know no faith nor law nor king. In the early dawn they crawl out of their wretched forest huts and destroy everything before them with fire and sword, pillaging the remotest corners of the Nakem Empire and driving the populations of those regions from their homes with no other recourse but to throw themselves on the mercy of Saif or to perish of hunger, sickness, and privation.

At that same time the Nakem provinces suffered such famine and pestilence that a very little food came to cost the price of a slave—at least three florins. Under the lash of necessity a father sold his son, a brother his brother; no villainy was too great if food might be procured by it. Those who were sold under pressure of starvation were bought by traders come from São Tomé in ships laden with food. The sellers claimed that these people were already slaves, and the sold, in their eagerness to be fed, were only too glad to concur. And so countless free men made slaves of themselves, sold themselves by necessity.

In almost every part of the Empire and its dependencies an unprecedented orgy of violence ensued. The capture of rebel tribes, of free men, of defeated warriors, the sacrifice of their chief and the feasting on his flesh, became ritual acts, which entered into the customs of those jittery jigs, whose barbarity fell in with the plans of the emperor and his notables. . . . Through intermediaries, Saif al-Haram encouraged the raiders to bless the wounded captives with a stroke of the saber, to carry their skulls spitted on lances and assegais to the door of the victor who—God wills it!—was·feasted as a hero. And as though a Black really had the soul of a man, the chief of the prisoners and his family were first given over to the mercies of the village women and children who whirled around them, leaping, dancing, singing, shouting insults, and spitting on them in order, so they swore, to cleanse their souls of Satan's blackness. On the third day of their captivity, the sorcerer, his eyes aflame with pride and avenging hate, skinned more than shaved their skulls, which were then rubbed with karite butter.

Then each villager in turn danced around the prisoners with a crudely carved wooden knife and "stabbed" the chief once for every year of his own age and once for every relative he himself had lost in the last slave raid. And before yielding his place to the next villager's blood lust, he bent his knee before the prisoner, taunted him and reviled him, spat on him and gave him three sharp blows, punctuated with a clicking of the tongue. And all laughed uproariously at the sight of the blood oozing from the victim's bruises.

On the night of the third day, his ankles weighed down with tinkling bells, the chief of the prisoners—bound hand and foot as the women whirled around him, lewdly uncovering their nakedness for a flashing moment, arching their backs and tapping their pubic hair with the palms of their hands—was castrated by the sorcerer amidst the ecstasy of the crowd, whose collective rejoicing verged on hysteria.

And paralyzed with pain, the castrated husband, his thighs sticky with blood, looked on helpless as his wives—first standing, but in that same instant rolled in the dust—became the harlots of the victorious village, stripped, and then to the mad rhythm of the tom-tom taken each in turn by every man and woman in the village. . . .

The next day but one, on the eve of the sacrifice, men and women were "purified" by bathing and massaged with cow butter (their children had been disemboweled immediately after the raid). On the seventh day of their captivity, they were rubbed with peanut oil and tied to a pole, half dead with pent-up rage under the taunting words and gestures of the villagers. Made feverish by the thought of their impending death, with burning eyes and foaming mouths, the captives butted the air with their heads and, frantic to kill their enemies, clawed and bit and snarled at them as they passed.

On the evening of this seventh day all the prisoners, glutted with palm wine, drunk on millet beer, were howling like dogs. At midnight they died on the wood fire, in the crackling hiss of their fat, presenting to the expert fingers of the cannibals human flesh as white as that of a suckling pig. The brains and the women's sexual parts were set aside for the "eminent men"; with clearly aphrodisiac intent, the chief's testicles were sprinkled with pepper and strong spice, to be relished by the women in their communal soup. Ordained by hatred, innate evil, blood lust, thirst for vengeance, or perhaps by a desire to inherit the qualities of the devoured victims, the ghoulish feast ended in an orgy of drinking. Cannibalism was one of the darkest features of that spectral Africa over which hung the malefic shadow of Saif al-Haram. A sob for her.

On April 20, 1532, on a night as soft as a cloak of moist satin, Saif al-Haram, performing his conjugal "duty" with his four stepmothers seriatim and all together, had the imprudent weakness to overindulge and in the very midst of his dutiful delights gave up the ghost. . . . The next day his raven-eyed minister Al Hadj Abd al-Hassana, having established a stripling boy and Hawa, the most beautiful of Saif's stepmothers, in his bed, was stung by an asp which he was caressing in the belief that he was holding something else, opened his mouth wide three times, and died. . . . His successor was his cousin Holongo, "a horrible biped with the brutal expression of a buffalo," humped in front and in back; after a reign of two years, moaning in enviable torment, he died in the arms of the courtesan Aiosha, who strangled him as he was crying out in ecstasy. His successor was Saif Ali, a pederast with pious airs, as vicious as a red donkey, who succumbed six months later to the sin of gluttony, leaving the crown to Saif Jibril, Ali's younger brother, who, slain by the sin of indiscretion, was replaced by Saif Yussufi, one of the sons of Ramina (mother of Saif al-Haram, got with child by her son at the cost of great effort). An albino notorious for his ugliness, he was twice felled by one of his wife's admirers; the third time —at last!—much to his amazement, he was carried off by an ill wind, ceding his place to Saif Medioni of Mostaganem, who was recalled to God ten days later, torn to pieces, so it is said, by the contrary angels of Mercy and Justice. Then the last children of the accursed Saif and of his stepmothers reigned successively: Saif Ezekiel, who was dethroned after four years; Saif Ismail, reduced to impotence for seven months, then forced to abdicate; and the third, Saif Benghighi of Saida, somnolent for five years: as though the Court were condemned to have no tongue but a forked one.

Years without glory, swallowing their shame in oblivion. And since all three of those Saifs seemed to have been born of a serpent—their accursed father—they awaited the coming of icy death empty-handed, without hope or courage. In Tillabéri-Bentia they had reached such a state of helplessness and dejection that they dozed from morning till night on the great square beneath the council tree, reduced to recalling the glorious days of the just Saif Isaac al-Heit. The perseverance with which they devoted themselves to grandiose dreams soon earned them Heaven's mild compassion: all in the same night they were carried away by . . . three asps. O tempora! O mores. . . .

. . . Accordingly, in 1546 the noble riffraff who had made it their business to dominate the Nakem people by bastardizing them, found themselves in the same precarious situation as in 1532, apparently doomed more than ever to ruin. *Mashallah! wa bismillah!* The name of Allah upon them and around them!

Amid unspeakable corruption the coffers were empty, and men weary in their hearts. In the hope of a black messiah, a Commander of the Faithful who would save the imperial tradition, the noble families of Rande province began to baptize their children by the name of Saif the Just, Saif Isaac al-Heit. To no avail, for in His infinite compassion the Eternal sent an epidemic of yellow fever which in less than a month destroyed all hopes, decimating the ranks of the pretenders to the throne. . . .

Hardened by this carnival of the divine will, bearing his turban like a halo, Saif Rabban Johanan ben Zakkai, last descendant of the accursed Saif, astride a horse that seemed to issue from his open fly, drew his cutlass, clove the luminous air of the dawn that lay on Tillabéri-Bentia, approached the bed of the evil spirits of the imperial Court, and with one blow dispatched the malefactors from sleep to death. Appointed emperor, he reveled for eight years in fresh-flowing honors and tamed the herd of envious notables. At the feast of Tabaski, wishing to savor his popularity amidst the acrid armpits of his subjects and the fragrant perfume of the ladies of the Court, he suddenly fell to the ground and kissed the dung-covered hoofs of his horse. "The evening dew moistened his temples," says the chronicle; "clutching the arrow that had pierced him, he had no time to say amen and to become a victim." A tear for him.

And so, assured that Saif Rabban Johanan ben Zakkai was one with the earth and equally asleep, the Gonda, lewdly cracking their finger joints, razed those mounds of clay, the huts of Saif's last remaining partisans, and flung themselves upon the throne.

For two hundred years courtiers, peasants, warriors, slaves, and artisans sang their praises, filling their pockets and swarming around the imperial cheese, in whose stench anyone with an ounce of ability could hope, in emulation of the Court, to obtain lands, cattle, titles of nobility, money, and everything it buys, including women.

Amidst all this turmoil, this dissolute life with its general bastardization, its vice and corruption, the Arab conquest, which had come several centuries earlier, settled over the land like a she-dog baring her white fangs in raucous laughter: more and more often, unfreed slaves and subjugated tribes were herded off to Mecca, Egypt, Ethiopia, the Red Sea, and America at prices as ridiculous as the flea-bitten dignity of the niggertrash.

A strong man in good health cost a little more than a she-goat and a little less than a he-goat, a tenth as much as a cow and an eighth as much as a camel, or, in currency, a thousand of the shells known as cowries, or two bars of salt. And (let us be grateful!) these far-flung commercial operations were masked by an apparent pursuit of spiritual values: Arab universities (few of which had existed hitherto) were established in Tillabéri-Bentia, Granta and Grosso, closely connected with the world of international commerce and the eastern slave trade.

The Empire was crumbling. . . . The Saif dynasty went from bad to worse with the grandsons of Saif Rabban Johanan, the eldest of whom, Jacob, so the griots relate, "spent his nights expounding all manner of abstruse theological problems to his cat." The animal's discretion was such that, to spare Jacob any excessive fear of the horrors that awaited him here below, it crept away at daybreak. After a brief sleep Jacob, clad in a simple dashiki, devoted himself to study and a scholar drummed wise precepts and noble sentiments into his mind with wand and cudgel. But since he was always silent, the Court found him pleasant and useless. When his father died, his brothers, not content to claim the throne, seized his share of their father's estate. And Jacob, with his tiny mouth that seemed to chirp under his beard, was obliged to live by their charity.

One day when he was sitting with his head sunk between his shoulders in the shade of the tree enclosing the green stone that makes men forget their troubles, he saw the imperial litter. It was a hot day; the litter carriers thought he had a willing look and asked him to help them. Jacob arose at once with a gentle smile, and after greeting the emperor his brother relieved one of the carriers. But the farther he went the more the litter was shaken. For Jacob hopped and jumped to avoid stepping on toads, ants, and other insects—he respected the life of the animals.

At length the emperor shouted at him:

"Idiot, can't you walk straight? Put down my litter at once."

Jacob looked at his brother Saif Tsevi, and answered in a voice as sweet as honey:

"To whom do you speak so rudely, calling him an idiot? Is there in Nakem, with its blue-glass sky and mother-of-pearl horizon—and the morning star overhead—anyone who is not yourself, and can there be anger in you?"

A great light flowed from Jacob's eyes as he spoke; those who heard him were filled with respect. The emperor descended from his litter and bowed before the wise man:

"God grant that I eat your sicknesses, venerable lord, my brother among the dead and the living!"

Then Jacob sat down by the roadside and for hours, wide-eyed and with countenance hungry for the supernatural, he taught the emperor Saif Tsevi the "true wisdom," and the emperor's heart beat in unctuous unison with his. . . .

But the blessed union of knowledge and morality is fragile, for shortly thereafter Saif Tsevi seduced his own sister and became her lover, and she in turn, once married and on the threshold of womanhood, became depraved, choosing her concubines with impunity among boys of ten. . . .

. . . After lamenting his Berbero-Jewish favorite Jehoshua, Saif Tsevi, an obstinate lecher, hastened to marry Lyangombe, a black sorceress belonging to a secret society of sorcerers and magicians, whose traditional ancestor was represented as a bisexual being—with three phalluses on one side and three vaginas on the other. In their private lives the members of that society, who had no more courage than a wet hen, observed a form of hospitality which rose above the general tragedy: a master of the house allowed all comers to enjoy his wives' favors.

In their public life they celebrated hideous sabbaths to which the members made their way through the bush at night, calling to one another with cries learned from the hyena. In those saturnalia incest was permitted and even recommended; human sacrifices were performed, followed by acts of incest and coitus with animals: as though a Black had no choice—*ya atrash*—but to be a savage.

The grand sorcerer and the grand sorceress bade the company sit down on the ground with legs parted; then, sweetly singing songs relating to the sex organs, they threw off all their clothes and copulated in public; weeping for joy in their indignity, they called on every man present to do the same with three, four, or five women, as many as their strength would permit and as often as possible. Saif Tsevi and his two other brothers, Sussan and Yossef, who—guided by the insolent penis of Satan—were present that night, were found by peddlers the next day, all three naked, their throats ripped open by the she-dogs they had been copulating with, which lay strangled in their arms.

After that the sole survivor of the male line of the Saifs was Jacob, who, as humble and wise as he was luminously poor, was counting the stars at the hour of his death eight years later. A desolation on his tomb.

―――――――

Yet amid this hideous hodgepodge of tribal custom, violence, and dilettantism embedded in the pious, feudal, idle, and voluptuous life of the Moslem landowners, a few powerful families survived: yes, they exercised power, but each in its limited sphere, a province, a district, a county. It was this fragmentation of authority that made the colonial conquest possible; patiently weathering the violence of the natives, it pressed forward, not on the basis of prearranged zones of influence or focal points, but at random, along lines of least resistance. The white man had spoken of a right to colonize—nay, more, of the "duty of international charity," the duty to bring "civilization," to suppress the slave trade that was devouring all Africa.

Later, addressing the people, Saif declared:

"No one denies the constructive aspects of colonization: but even the greatest of its benefits, education for instance, brought grave evils in their train, so-called assimilation, contempt for native culture, etc. Moreover, one cannot help wondering whether these benefits are not due rather to a beginning of decolonization than to colonization itself. Universal suffrage, labor laws, self-determination, a more equitable distribution of the profits between the colonizers and the colonized, are the fruits not of colonialism but of the struggle against colonialism."

For at the very moment when the inexorable white man was embarking on the conquest of Africa, the chiefs of the Randigue, Gonda, Fulani, Ngodo, and certain lesser tribes promised to respect each other's independence, and to cease all raids and warfare. But once this new state of affairs had been achieved—practice makes perfect—the same chiefs, wishing to consolidate their power now that all was peaceful, donned the mask of progressivism. They promised their serfs, servants, and former captives that, pending the hostilities which the neighboring tribe was no doubt plotting, they would be "looked upon— hear!—as provisionally free and equal subjects." Then, once peace was restored among the various tribes, for the war had failed to break out—hee-hee—the same notables promised the same subjects that after . . . hum . . . hum . . . a brief "apprenticeship" of forced labor, they would be rewarded with the Rights of Man. . . . As to civil rights, of them no mention was made. Hallelujah!

Thus in every province of the Nakem Empire, now dismembered by a multitude of kinglets who aped one another, forced labor became the mainstay of economic life. The religious aristocracy, however (in co-operation with the notables), proclaimed to the overjoyed populace that forced labor was at an end, replaced by "voluntary labor," which would bring them all —bing! *iru turu inè turu*—"true freedom and full citizenship." . . .

Accordingly, each aristocrat, each notable, allotted—what could be more democratic?—a parcel of land to his serfs, who would till the whole estate "for the salvation of their souls."

Thus, eighteen years before the arrival of the Whites, thirty years after the birth, in the maternal line of the Saifs, of Saif ben Isaac al-Heit (that is, Saif son of Isaac al-Heit)—the notables recalled the people to the "supreme values of peace, order, and tradition, luminously exemplified by God Himself."

. . . In anticipation of the great and not too distant day when a world would dawn in which a serf would be the equal of a king, the niggertrash—dogs that bite, leash them tight!—accepted whatever came their way. Forgive us, O Lord. *Amba, koubo oumo agoum.*

Pillar of the Nakem Empire, Saif ben Isaac al-Heit—who, so it is said, resembled his ancestor Saif Isaac al-Heit in every feature—was a staunch believer in the above-mentioned principle of *spiritual advancement*. With the support of the sheikhs, emirs, and ulemas, he formed a union of the aristocrats and notables throughout the Empire who, setting aside their lemon-yellow babouches at the doors of the mosques, practiced Islam with great humility and converted the fetishist populace who were beginning to be dismayed at the blackness of their souls. This made it still easier to hold down the people and exploit them. And the Evil One shall be driven out!

Having depopulated whole regions, the slave trade had long been unprofitable and seeped away like water in the hungry sand. It had become difficult to find good laborers, and all in all it seemed preferable to bleed the people with all manner of taxes, direct and indirect, drive them to the utmost in the fields and workshops of the notables at a meager wage for which the Hereafter would find means to compensate them. The religious gymnastics of the five daily prayers of Islam were maintained as a safety valve; the poor in mind and spirit were kept busy searching and striving for Allah's Eternal Kingdom. Religion, whose soul had been vomited by the clergy of Nakem, became a deliberately confused mumbling about human dignity, a learned mystification; losing its mystical content, it became a means of action, a political weapon. Marabouts and notables battened on it, entered into sumptuous polygamous marriages with the leading families of the day, merging their interests and thronging in pilgrimage to Mecca, the Holy City. Intelligence is a gift of the God who metes out rewards: *wassalam*.

In reality the nobility, warriors in the days of the first Saifs (Glory to the Almighty God), had become intriguers for power: Amen. At the death of the accursed Saif (Blessed be the Eternal One!), conscious of their own need of stability (So be it!), they had flung the people into a bath of pseudo-spirituality, while enslaving them materially. (And praised.)

Had the Imam Mahmud, grand sherif of Mecca, not predicted that in the thirteenth century of the Hegira a caliph would come from Tekrur? And was this caliph not Saif ben Isaac al-Heit, whose mother, "that the commandments of the Eternal One might be fulfilled," had arranged to bring him into the world and baptize him in Tekrur on the date foreseen by the prophecy and the legend? . . .

Luckily for Saif, he played the messiah well, for in that same role countless scions of the aristocracy had run themselves ragged and emptied their pockets in vain. Not every man can be Christ. Forgive us, O Lord, for revering so assiduously the cults in which men have clothed Thee. . . .

. . . Sponsored by the banks, the universities, the Army and the Navy—geographical societies, international associations of philanthropists, explorers, economists, and promoters sprang up throughout Europe, unleashing a deadly competition between the European powers which swarmed through Nakem, fighting, conquering, pacifying, obtaining treaties, and burying cartridges, gunflints, bullets, and gunpowder in token of peace. "We are burying war so deep," they said, "that our children will not be able to dig it up again. The tree that will grow here will bear witness to the everlasting alliance between Whites and Blacks. And until the day when its branches bear bullets, cartridges, and gunpowder, peace will endure."

There followed a rush for that precious raw material, the niggertrash. The Whites devised a system of international colonial law consecrating the principle of spheres of influence and legitimizing the rights of the first occupant. But to Nakem the colonial powers came too late, for with the help of the local notables a colonial overlord had established himself long since, and that colonial overlord was none other than Saif. All unsuspecting, the European conquerors played into his hands. Call it technical assistance. At that early date! So be it! Thy work be sanctified, O Lord. And exalted.

TWO

# Ecstasy and Agony

How in profound displeasure, with perfumed mouth and eloquence on his tongue, Saif ben Isaac al-Heit endeavored to mobilize the energies of the fanatical people against the invader; how to that end he spread reports of daily miracles throughout the Nakem Empire—earthquakes, the opening of tombs, resurrections of saints, fountains of milk springing up in his path, visions of archangels stepping out of the sunset, village women drawing buckets from the well and finding them full of blood; how on one of his journeys he transformed three pages of the "Holy Book," the Koran, into as many doves, which flew on ahead of him as though to summon the people to Saif's banner; and with what diplomacy he feigned indifference to the goods of this world: in all that there is nothing out of the ordinary.

Yet the fact remains that for all his subtleties and refinements —Allah protect him from the evil eye!—the supernatural proved inadequate and he was obliged to revive a military art that had fallen into disuse.

Assegais, lances, poisoned arrows, javelins, machetes, daggers, sabers and muskets, weapons of every kind, all thrice

blessed by Saif ben Isaac al-Heit, were issued to the warriors of
Nakem, Nakem-Ziuko, Goro Foto Zinko, Yame, Geboue, and
Katsena, to the Sao, the Galibi, the Gohu, the Gonda, the Dar-
gol, and the Ngodo; at the same time, riding black mules, sorcerers, charmers of vipers and boas, magi, criminals specializing
in ordalic murder, herborists expert in poisoning and in the
treatment of wells and ponds, assassins versed in the use of ven-
omous plants, lethal objects, and terrifying animals, thronged to
the banner of country and religion: fetishes, warriors, snakes,
bees, wasps, arrows, elephants, panthers—these were the tanks
of the Nakem resistance.

More than a hundred of the invader's scouts exploded from
sipping the water of poisoned ponds; terrified at the sight, countless black soldiers deserted from the army of the Whites. They
were killed with poisoned darts, spies took their guns, powder,
and shot and put on their uniforms, which enabled them, unde-
tected, to sabotage the advancing column and observe its line of
march.

The warriors blessed by Saif—who held out his sword to the
right of him and opened up a passage as wide as a village street
—thought themselves invulnerable; with fury painted on their
faces, thousands of them went home to the old moons; but, so it
was said, "they did not die, they went to meet the Most-High."
*Djallè! Djallè! Amoul bop! Makoul fallè!*

And that is why the night goes on, whiter than the face of
day.

The long line of officers and men drag themselves painfully
over the trails choked with weeds. They all try to appear calm
and collected, but Africa is there, in ambush. Winter had
brought a brief truce between resistants and foreign troops, but
early in 1898 the foreigners had invaded Groure and Nieke,
coastal territories densely populated and rich, where gold dust
is hidden in the hollows of elephants' tusks, in ivory knick-
knacks, or in little antelope horns set in red leather.

In every province black resistants carry off black captives and
with this currency purchase horses, powder, and weapons, so

swelling the perpetual files of slaves. And meanwhile the Whites gain ground.

They pillage, loot, destroy everything in their path—the captives, some eight thousand of them, are herded together and the colonel, writing in his little black book, starts to apportion them. But then he gives up and shouts: "Go on, divide 'em up."

And each white man chooses for himself more than ten black women. Return to base with captives in daily marches of twenty-five miles. The children, the sick and disabled are killed with rifle butts and bayonets, their corpses abandoned by the roadside. A woman is found squatting. Big with child. They push her, prod her with their knees. She gives birth standing up, marching. The umbilical cord is cut, the child kicked off the road, and the column marches on, heedless of the delirious whimpering mother, who, limping and staggering, finally falls a hundred yards farther on and is crushed by the crowd.

Time passes; once more tornadoes send down sheets of water, roads and trails are drowned in mud. The Yame River swells and floods the low-lying plains.

The Blacks requisitioned en route to carry provisions go five whole days without rations—forty lashes if one of them filches a handful of food from the twenty to fifty pounds that he carries on his bare, shaved head. The *tirailleurs,* the common soldiers, the noncoms and officers all have so many slaves they are unable to count, lodge, or feed them. When they get to Gagol-Gosso, which has surrendered, they ask for food and huts for their slaves; the Chief's answer: "Sell them." They sold them. Those whom nobody wanted were drowned to save ammunition. And the march continued, a nightmare: towns and villages resisted, attacking the columns in the rear by night, loosing swarms of bees and showers of poisoned or flaming arrows, encircling the enemy in a sheath of fire.

But all this was merely a volley of pinpricks, which did not prevent the Whites from rallying, sending out their shock troops —black *tirailleurs*—and razing the villages after the soldiers had sacked them.

In the course of those raids, fields and harvests were laid

waste, populations sold into slavery, and innumerable half-breeds brought into the world and abandoned at birth. Not the least astonishing by-product of those horrors was the following:

Relatives of black *tirailleurs,* persons devoted to the White cause, were occasionally given away or sold by mistake. To repair such blunders, innumerable "passes" were made out to family members. "Moussa is authorized to go to Granta with one man and one little girl (not free) to redeem the relative of a notable of Gagol-Gosso. . . ." "Ali is authorized to go to Zemba to look for a captive by the name of Niamba Kimane, given to Amala, an auxiliary in Borgnis Desborde's company who took part in the attack on the city of Buanga-Fele. . . ."

And yet, at infrequent intervals, a caravan traversed those dismal and endless plains: slave traders driving wretched files of men, women, and children, covered with open sores, choked in iron collars, their wrists shackled and bleeding.

In serried flight, crows, buzzards, bald vultures with long bare necks, follow the caravan, sure of feasting at every halt on the bodies of those who will die, weakened by their wounds and their bowels twisted by hunger; and on those who will be abandoned alive because their feet, worn to the bone by sores and fatigue, can carry them no farther. . . . Throughout the High Rande and the Yame as well, to the north and south of the Great River, from Krotti-Bentia to Dangabiara, there is no road or trail that is not punctuated with such stopping places, places of death and crime, vestiges of the only commerce which, under the white man's protection, flourishes in those regions. . . . All persons of good faith familiar with that country agreed that a caravan of so-called slaves of war, guided by natives or not, lost roughly a third of its cargo of human flesh en route to the market or staging center.

The "friendly" villages through which the caravans passed were *only* obliged to supply food, beasts of burden, and able-bodied men. These last were used as porters and often abandoned without resources hundreds of miles away. Therefore everlasting glory and infinite praise to the God of Rewards, the master of joy, intelligence, and happiness. Amen.

The following year the invaders laid siege to the fortress of Saif ben Isaac al-Heit, who one dark night in August 1900 left his palace of Tillabéri-Bentia and beat a hasty retreat in the direction of Kikassougou, which degenerated into a rout. Abandoning more than eight hundred horses, four hundred camels, and a thousand asses, he drove herds and famished populations before him, leaving only ruins and desolation behind. Disaster hovered over the legions in flight and rebellion seethed in their midst; every tattooed man—tattooed, that is, not on the forehead (the tattoo of the Saifs) but on the temples—could reasonably expect to be murdered. Now that race warfare had been unleashed, the savage, bloodthirsty Saif resumed his expeditions of rapine in the direction of the Yame River. Sick of the continual massacres, whole villages, their huts in flames, threw themselves on the protection of the Flencessi* and blessed it, while Saif invaded the Tetenoubou with his faithful guard and attacked Doukkamar.

In the presence of his assembled griots, Saif swore to bring back the heads of the white leaders, and the very next day he marched off to war. Two emissaries from Saif went to the Gonda in the city of Toma, who had been apprised of their coming; "Submit to Saif, or, by Allah, your country will be laid waste, your father and mother burned alive, and your sons executed."

Ali, the Gonda chief of Toma, a warrior of great renown—his ancestors in times gone by had defeated the Saifs and the Dia, and he himself had been wounded twenty times in battle with the Mossi—replied: *"Wallahi!* by my head and by my eye! Tell Saif that if he is the stronger he will take my country; but I will defend it to the blood of the last of my children: *wassalam!* Besides, I've sworn to the French that I will never surrender to the impious Saif."

And so, faithful to its tradition of tribal warfare, the old Empire was tearing itself to pieces in massacres; over areas of hun-

* The French.

dreds of square miles, missions were sacked and burned, the missionaries slaughtered by the emperor, who spitted the white men's heads on lances and assegais.

Stopped outside of Toma, Saif said: "We must drive three white sheep and seven white chickens to the ramparts. If the fetish animals enter the fortress alive, it means that our attack will be successful. . . ."

This return to paganism was amazingly effective; it rallied all the animists of the region, who flocked to the camp by the tens of thousands and poisoned the drinking water of countless French troops, who were thus paralyzed. At the sight of the chickens and sheep, Ali knew that Saif would attack in force. Ordering three thousand men to gather wood, he lit an enormous bonfire; six hundred muskets fired first three, then seven volleys through the swirls of smoke: an exorcism.

When the smoke came toward them driven by the wind, the three white sheep and seven white chickens beat a retreat; at the same time Saif's men heard the volleys of musket fire.

Infuriated by the exorcism, a sorcerer fired a rifle at Saif, who at that very moment turned toward smoking Toma and unwittingly avoided the bullet, which blew out the brains of his master-at-arms. To avenge him, one of Saif's officers flung his javelins at the sorcerer, gravely wounding him and killing his horse, which fell with its head transpierced.

At this seventeen thousand faithful warriors withdrew to their camp, and hundreds more followed until nearly the whole army had gone. The withdrawal went on for an hour. And Saif cried out:

"Give me an army, I ask no more. An army! . . . The subjects of my Empire have risen against me, seeking refuge with those apes in helmets. An army and I'll send those white apes packing."

. . . But History has mysteries compounded of silence, cowardice, and slow-moving tragedy, followed by appeasement and sudden about-faces. Aware that all was lost, Saif, on foot in the bush some thousands of paces from Toma, suddenly drew his sword and swung it whistling through the air in a quarter circle, meaning to bring it down on his own throat: his son came running and the cold steel descended on his head, which fell to the earth like a sheaf of grain. This disaster, more than anything else, made Saif's weariness complete. The very next day he surrendered.

The Empire was pacified, broken up into several zones which the Whites divided. Saved from slavery, the niggertrash welcomed the white man with joy, hoping he would make them forget the mighty Saif's meticulously organized cruelty.

. . . Saif was returned under military escort to his palace in Tillabéri-Bentia. As the marabouts prayed and the griots in the courtyard sang his praises, the emperor, his sole-remaining younger son at his right side, ordained silence and, on that twentieth day of December 1900, awaited the peace treaty he was to sign.

Surrounded by a court as magnificent as in the days of his glory, clothed in the imperial insignia, he sat on his throne; his feet rested on satin carpets embroidered with golden flowers. Over his short tunic he wore a large, richly embossed dashiki, open at the throat; from his neck hung two fetishes; on his head a fez surrounded by a jet-black turban; on his legs dark trousers and on his feet Moorish boots with hippopotamus hide soles.

Raising his arms, he set upon his head a golden diadem whose points were studded with pearls. Soberly but richly clad, his loyal retinue were more dejected than usual, their eyes submerged in the darkness of dreams.

Forgetting the salaam, Saif did not rise to greet the French delegation, but merely motioned them to be seated. Behind the emperor, two masters-at-arms, dressed all in red, thrust their assegais into the ground and stood motionless in an attitude of barbaric nobility, their arms extended as though to swear an oath. In their left hands they held a sharpened ax and a silver mace fastened with lion hide, the emblem of royalty. Two gleaming muskets were slung over their shoulders. On their faces they wore masks made from the skin of the king of beasts.

To the right and left Saif's twenty-seven favorite wives, all young and exquisite, clad in silks and heavy brocades. At the rear sixty serving-women and forty manservants, all captives and sons of captives, devoted to Saif. Behind them the children, squatting on mats. In a semicircle roundabout, the royal guard of six hundred warriors with bells on their arms and ankles, and copper rings in their right ears.

Slowly Saif moved his eyes over the assemblage; his soul became thinner than a thread and, grave in his helplessness, he signed the treaty. Glory to the Only Living One!

Six months later the Flencessi invited Madoubo, his younger son, to visit their country. Saif accepted in the following terms:

"A thousand greetings. . . . May these thanks be sweeter to you than honey and sugar; they are addressed to your valiant people, the sight of whom here rejoices our eyes, whose presence is as pleasing to our hearts as the fruit of the tree, and dispels their sorrows."

That was Saif: In confirmation of a good faith and friendly sentiments that did not exist, he entrusted his son to the homeward-bound French delegation.

The Lord, holy is His Name, willed Madoubo's arrival in France, and especially in Paris, to be a great event. He was welcomed by the leading lights of the government. He marveled at the Elysée palace, the Arch of Triumph, and the crowds on the Grands Boulevards, and on July 14, 1901, he attended the military review at Longchamp.

The band played; within a circle of solemn staff officers resplendent with medals and braid, decorations were awarded. Madoubo was overwhelmed: "It was like a chasm of light," he said, "a sky upside down." The charge of the cavalry on their black horses and white horses so filled him with enthusiasm—for each passing day renewed his astonishment woven of innocence—that he asked leave to take a cuirassier's uniform home with him.

The curiosity mingled with admiration which the son of Saif aroused in the Parisians called to mind—so the papers reported—the visit of Aniaba, son of the King of Assinia, to the Court of

Louis XIV. The young prince had immediately won Bossuet's heart; he was baptized and the King, after standing godfather, had commissioned him an officer. Then one morning news had come that the King of Assinia was dead. Cardinal de Noailles performed a kind of coronation ceremony for Aniaba at Notre-Dame, and on the day of his departure Louis XIV said to him: "Now there is no other difference between you and me than the difference between black and white."

Governor-General Delavignette commented on these words as follows: "The words of Louis XIV to Prince Aniaba seem today to take on a new timeliness, for they strike at the essence of present developments in Africa. When Louis XIV said to Aniaba: 'Now there is no other difference between you and me than the difference between black and white,' he meant that both were kings, brothers in kingship, and that, though differing in color, they were united by the identity of their royal nature. And now, by extension, there is an identity of royal nature between Africa and ourselves."

Frantic applause rang out and all Paris rejoiced. Presents were heaped upon the son of Saif, who, now become a symbol of Franco-African co-operation, returned to his illustrious father.

On his return to Nakem, Madoubo found that his father had not been idle; he had populated his palace with twenty-three newborn babes conceived by twenty of his twenty-seven wives.

An unforeseen consequence: on Madoubo's return the popular imagination transformed defeat into genius and the dictatorship of a tyrannical dynasty into eternal glory; the defeated emperor was numbered among the cohorts of "those just men whose greatness quenches the thirst of the agonizing heart." *La illaha illallah, la illaha, illaha! mahamadara souroulaio* . . .

Twilight of the gods? Yes and no. More than one dream seemed to be fading; a turning point of civilization, or should one say a convulsion presaging its ultimate end? Presaging a new birth? Or merely a sempiternal agony, presaging nothing? A tear for the niggertrash, O Lord, in Thy compassion! . . .

# The Night of the Giants

1

The sole vestige of those abortive dreams—the venom is in the tail!—was the serf whose days of hard labor closely resembled those of a convict.

Get up at five in the morning to prepare the master's bath before he goes to the mosque; run to open the door while the silent-stepping slave women busy themselves with breakfast: couscous, mutton sauce, milk, sugar, fritters. Go down to the Yame River in the stillness of dawn to draw water for the day.

Supervise the three women who sweep the courtyard while five others crush millet to make milk porridge for the peasant slaves who till the master's lands. Collect the washing, soiled in the last two days; issue soap to the laundresses and send them to the river. Prepare baths for the twenty-seven wives of the lord and master; instruct their serving-women to hear and obey; help them to wash. Help the mistresses of the house to select a dress, a shift, a loincloth, a shawl, a tunic, which to their chagrin they must wear twice instead of changing every day. Spin cotton or wool; put away the skeins and distaffs; take the thread to the weaver, come back; give the ladies an accounting, to which they hardly listen; run off on some errand but be recalled halfway for a less urgent task. Pick banana or cola leaves to wrap the hands and feet of the twenty-seven mistresses, who dye them with henna, the indispensable nail polish. . . . Then stand aside.

For, in accordance with the custom of the country, all those aristocrats had their breakfast without talking or even drinking.

The male captives wait at a distance. Then they clear away the dishes, wash them, and eat their own food in haste.

They clean the stables, take out the dung, change the grass of the horses' troughs which, so the rules require, must be always fresh and juicy.

The women captives wash the dishes of the male captives and breakfast in their turn. At last. Daybreak. It is seven o'clock.

Litter, mats, couches, beds, mosquito netting, sheets, blankets —everything is in order. The reward: an hour's rest.

Then each one goes to make his bow, pay his compliments to the lord and his wives, and wish them a good day.

The neighborhood notables come calling. The lords and notables exchange visits and discuss the latest news.

The serfs chat among themselves in small isolated groups, then return to their courtyards.

Twenty serfs and the new recruits go to the fields with the peasant slaves.

At the head of ten serving-women, Tambira goes to market to sell the master's milk, a hundred quarts or more. Assisted by three other serfs, Kassoumi, the slave-cook bought from the marabout Al Hadj Hassan, loads the house donkeys with seventeen sacks of cola nuts which will be sold wholesale that very morning at the market: such is Saif's will. After which they will go out to the pasture, slaughter an ox from Saif's herd, cut up the meat, load it on the donkeys, and bring it to the kitchen after having emptied and washed the intestines in the Yame River. After selling the hide to the local shoemaker or to the blacksmith for his bellows and handing over the money to his master at ten o'clock sharp, Kassoumi supervises the grilling of the fillets and the cooking of the roasts, and distributes among the servants the meat needed for the master's table. Then comes the share of the serfs, captives, and slaves, depending on how much meat, entrails, bone, and gristle is left.

At about one in the afternoon, one day when he was off duty, Kassoumi went for a walk. A hot, sticky day. The sun coiled like a spring, ready to strike whosoever should venture out into the hail of its motionless might.

On leaving the courtyard of the slaves, Kassoumi had turned to the right; his misery in tow, he crossed Tillabéri-Bentia with quick gangling steps. After passing the last houses, he relaxed his pace and turned down the dusty path that leads to the Yame River.

He felt small, alone, empty, lost in his coat that was too big for him; its sleeves covered his hands, its tails got in the way of his gray, baggy trousers, obliging him to spread his legs when he was in a hurry. He was barefoot. The dreary weary look of an unpaid worker, and in his large black eyes a gentleness and an almost animal simplicity; on his right eyelid a birthmark.

He didn't seem to feel the sun, he moved as though pursuing an idea, a meeting with himself, for he had found a spot in the shade of a banana tree, which reminded him of his home, and it was only in that spot that he felt happy.

Where the paths end and footprints lose themselves in the sandy bank, he took off the hat which squeezed his temples and wiped his forehead. Out of breath, he stopped for a while on a hummock, as though to get used to the sun, pale quicksilver caressing the water. There his body remained for a moment or two, afire with the phosphorescence of the afternoon, while his mind, haunted by vague memories of his home country—childish imaginings—recaptured a bit of field, a hedge, a hut, a mother, a far-away slave raid, the palace of the Saifs.

At the edge of the woods he picked a fig banana and, thinking of the people at home, slowly peeled off the ribs of skin. From time to time his monotone voice uttered a name, recalled an incident in his childhood; a few syllables sufficed to kindle a memory. And little by little that distant country invaded him, bridging the distance to send him its shapes, its sounds, its familiar horizons, its smells, and the taste of the green earth in the breeze.

He sat down under his banana tree, happy and sad, filled with the slow, penetrating sorrow of a caged beast that remembers. So he remained, silent and melancholy, with a humming in his temples, his fingers crossed as in the presence of his master, his black legs outstretched in the meadow grass. The whiteness of his dashiki and the metal of his saber stopped the chirping sparrows that had been flitting about over his head.

Turning toward Tillabéri-Bentia, he saw Tambira, who was coming down the river. Her parted lips were pressed against the hairy skin of a frond, and Kassoumi was gladdened by the amber glints of her calabash laundry basket under the flame of the sun.

She was a tall, robust woman, black and supple; catching sight of him, her fine almond-shaped eyes laughed with the protective benevolence of an experienced woman conscious of Kassoumi's timidity.

"What are you doing here?" she asked. "Are you watching the bananas grow?"

"That might be it," he answered gaily.

"Yééé rêti," she said. "It's hot."

And he, still laughing: "That's the truth."

She started off again, but after a few yards she changed her mind and came back: "Maybe you have some washing to be done? I'm doing mine."

"No, thank you," said Kassoumi, but he was pleased. She stood for a moment before him, her hands on her hips, her calabash balanced on her head, happy at the pleasure her offer had given him.

With a "good-by, see you again," she left him.

He followed her with his eyes; her silhouette grew smaller and smaller and seemed to sink into the pale ocher of the sand.

On the following Friday she saw him sitting in the same place:

"Greetings, Kassoumi."

"Greetings, Tambira. May your path be straight."

"May God hear you and reward you. Do you always come here?"

Kassoumi stammered happily: "Yes . . . I come here to rest."

That was all. But the Friday after that she laughed when she saw him, her eyes sparkled like the stars, her smile spread like a ray of sunlight, and pointing her finger at something she had in the calabash, she asked him diffidently: "Would you like some? It will remind you of home."

With the instinct of one of like race—she too no doubt was far from home—she had guessed right. Both were silent. Not without difficulty she poured a little honey into a small wooden bowl that she had wrapped in a clean white cloth; Kassoumi drank first, taking tiny little sips, stopping every second to make sure he wasn't taking more than what he reckoned to be his share. Then he passed the bowl to Tambira.

She lapped up the honey bit by bit, rolling it with her tongue from one cheek to another. Sitting across from her, he watched her with tenderness and delight.

Then she put the bowl away.

She sat down beside him to chat awhile, and both of them, side by side, abandoned themselves to the intoxication of feeling alive. Clasping their knees in their arms, they told each other all about the villages where they were born, while in its calabash, which she had set down on the ground, the washing reminded them that they would soon have to part.

But then the girl consented to eat a few bananas with him and to drink a little goat's milk which he poured from his pouch.

. . . They took to bringing each other sweets, for it was the time of the millet harvest, and fritters of all kinds were made in the house of the Saifs. That providential spot brought the two slaves to life, and when they were there they chirped like two sparrows.

# The Night of the Giants

One Thursday Kassoumi asked permission to leave the house for a few hours—something he had never done. He seemed very strange, agitated, and quite unlike himself. Saif did not understand, but vaguely suspected something, he didn't know what.

The slave went to his usual spot, where he had sat so much that the grass was worn away, and stayed awhile, deep in thought. Then, making a long detour, he approached the Yame River and hid behind a tree.

Suddenly he saw her.

The light of the moon seemed to flow from her sweet body and the radiance of the sun from her face. She had necklaces on her breasts and on her hair a kerchief; a hundred beads clung to her arms and legs and came together in a bow at the waist.

She walked with a slight swaying motion, as though carried by a skiff, seeming to curtsy nimbly at every step. He could not take his eyes off her and was seized with an overwhelming desire for this woman. His back broke out in a cold sweat, and he was filled with a dull rage, a helpless anger. But then, brusquely assuming an air of detachment, he tried with gentle gestures to bring himself to reason, to forget his madness.

Guided by the silver-eyed sun, she walked on. And he, with trembling lips and eyes aflame, listened to himself as he watched her.

Far and wide there was no one. Nothing stirred. Not a bird's cry nor the chirping of a cricket, not a sound, not even a lapping of water, the river lay stunned beneath the weight of the sun. But in the scorching air Kassoumi seemed to hear a humming of fire.

She disappeared behind a bush; then suddenly he sensed a slight movement behind one of the rocks half immersed in the silent water; rising on tiptoes, he saw Tambira, naked and broad-hipped, taking her bath, confident of being quite alone at that torrid hour. The water rose barely to her thighs—Heaven bless her!

Her head was turned toward the Yame and her body in tears was covered with watery suns: Eve in the crystal-clear water, under the shimmering light. She was marvelously beautiful, tall, statuesque. And the caressing sun nibbled at her insolent, swollen breasts.

She turned around, screamed, and, half swimming, half walking, hid behind her rock.

Kassoumi sat down against the tree and waited; she'd have to come out sometime. After a while she showed her head; her hair sent up rows of tapers, whose bristling suggested a porcupine or the tentacles of a jellyfish. Her wide, firm lips opened over dazzling white teeth, and her questioning eyes brought out the velvet softness of her skin—the color of old mahogany, firm and desirable, burnished by the blood-kindling air of the Yame.

"Go away!" she cried out. Her deep vibrant voice had a troubling guttural note. That voice became her as the sunbeam becomes the mountain, as dew becomes the fresh grass. Kassoumi didn't stir. "It's not nice of you to stay there." The syllables crackled like the yelping of a dog. Kassoumi didn't stir. The head disappeared.

After the time it takes to walk a hundred paces, the tapers reappeared, then the rest of her hair, then the forehead, then the eyes, slowly and circumspectly like a child playing hide-and-seek.

Now she seemed furious. "You're giving me a sunstroke," she cried. "I won't come out until you've gone."

Then Kassoumi stood up and, regretfully, feeling very sorry for himself, turned his back and went away, not without frequent glances behind him. When she thought he had gone far enough, she slipped out of the water, half bent over, swaying at the hips, her body streaming with life; her back was turned to him; and she disappeared behind a wave, behind a bush, behind a shift that was hanging from it.

The next day, Friday, Kassoumi went back. She was bathing again, the rascal, but this time she was all dressed. As lively as a deer, she pranced with malicious merriment and clucked for joy. Her joy laughed for the sun, danced for the moon; he was vexed and went away. He sat down under his banana tree, put his cap on his knees as though his head needed air, and spoke aloud in the silence: "She's a beautiful woman, all right." He thought of her again that night as he lay on his mat and in the morning when he woke up. He felt neither sad nor put out, there was some strange thing inside him, he didn't know what. Something that tormented him, that gripped his soul, a yearning that wouldn't go away, an indefinable stirring in his heart, something he couldn't catch or chase away or stifle. He was obsessed and on edge; the thought of Tambira filled him, he felt driven toward her by his whole heart and body. He wanted to hold her, to crush her, to take her into himself. In his rage he shook with a sense of impotence, with impatience and irritation, because she did not belong to him.

One Friday afternoon she stopped under his banana tree. It was hot. The grass all about them had grown high after the harvest. She had done her washing and was just coming up from the river, clad only in a short shift which molded her loins when she raised her arms to hold her calabash—delight! Balancing with the pole of time, his soul walked a tightrope; it danced over her body as on a rope stretched over the void of his own. The shock took his breath away, he thought her so desirable that the world swam before his eyes. He made her sit down. The time had come to speak.

"Look, Tambira," he stammered, "it can't go on like this."

"What?" she asked with a pathetic look, a look of gentle dismay. "What can't go on like this?"

And he replied: "That I think of you as many hours as the day is long."

Forcing a smile, she said in a very natural voice: "That's not my fault."

"Oh yes . . . yes, it is," he stammered: "you've stolen my sleep, my peace, my appetite, everything. . . ."

Half surprised, she turned to Kassoumi with grave alarm in her dark eyes: "Wh . . . what can be done to cure you?"

He sat there bewildered, his arms dangling: "Oh, my sun . . . oh, my light!"

Just above the banana tree, flitting over the dense screen of tall grass, a bird burst into song. It sang in trills and runs—piercing notes that seemed to merge with the horizon, to roll along the riverbank and seep away through the trees.

They were close together, their eyes lost in memories, their lips tense: and slowly, between their throbbing lips, they sucked the silence. Kassoumi put his arm around Tambira's waist and pressed her gently. Without anger, she took hold of his hand and pushed it back whenever he thrust it forward, but she felt no embarrassment; his caress was something perfectly natural, which it was just as natural for her to rebuff. Lost in ecstasy, she listened to the bird. An infinite yearning for happiness, a sudden tenderness came over her—revelations of unsuspected poetry; trembling, she felt her heart and nerves dissolve, and she pressed the man's hand. Now he was holding her close; she no longer resisted him, she didn't even dream of it.

So they stayed for some time. Suffused with sweet sensations, the woman was silent. Kassoumi's head rested on her shoulder. Suddenly he kissed her lips. Furiously she recoiled and sprang back to avoid him. He toppled her over. She pulled down her dress over her thighs and tried to escape. He flung himself down on her, covering her with his whole body, he was scratched, battered, harassed by the leather of her heaving breasts. Her mouth evaded him, but at last he found it and fastened his own to it. Then, maddened, she caressed him, clinging to his loins and returning his kiss; filled with a delicious sensation of defeat, she felt her resistance fall away as though crushed by too heavy a weight.

The leaves murmured as a light breeze brushed over them; naked in the tall grass, they mingled their sighs in consent. Transfigured and half delirious, conscious of nothing but their possession of each other, of their profound penetration, they lay enlaced, saturated with the mingling of their bodies, the drunkenness of their movements, raving, panting, tense from head to foot with passionate expectation. The woman carried the man as the sea carries a ship, with a light rocking motion, which rises and falls, barely suggesting the violence below. In the course of their voyage they sobbed and murmured; their movements accelerated, generating an unbearable force. The man groaned, he allowed his weapon to go faster, deeper, stronger between the woman's thighs. The venom spurted; and suddenly they felt suffocated, on the point of explosion or death—an instant of intolerable joy, chaste and wanton—terrifying.

They awoke from it vibrant, maddened, silent; weary and drained, with a humming in their ears; sated, obsessed, for they still felt possessed one by the other.

From that day on they met in the ditches, in hollows in the fields, in the tall grass under the banana tree, or else on the riverbank at dusk, when he was bringing back the donkeys laden with tanned hides or beef and she was returning from the river with water or the washing.

It was only natural that tongues should wag among the slaves. . . . Everyone said they were made for each other. When Saif heard of it, he promised they would be married the following month, so transforming the respectful hatred of the serfs into adoration: the heartbeat of the people knows strange irregularities.

Egged on by Saif, the supervisors Wagouli, Kratonga, and Sankolo, and the agents Wampoulo and Yafolè increased the chores of the domestics. They performed them cheerfully, little suspecting that the marriage of Tambira and Kassoumi was only a trick of the wily master, whose affectation of paternalism was highly profitable to him. *Alif minpitjè!*—and exalted be the God of Glory. . . .

Two weeks before the date set for the marriage, the military commander of Krebbi-Katsena—who had jurisdiction over the French colony of Nakem—invited Saif to an inauguration ceremony in the court of honor of the newly completed administration buildings on Mt. Katsena. Present were native notables and dignitaries, and representatives of the French civil and military establishment. Amid great pomp the superior officers welcomed the governor, his family, and forty-three new arrivals from France: Abbé Henry and seven missionaries, some officers, the wives of ten colonists, and a group of adventurers, politicians, idealists, and civil servants.

Then in the afternoon, when Bishop Thomas de Saignac disembarked in Nakem, Saif, the governor, and the entire population welcomed him amid indescribable joy. For a distance of three miles from the Yame River to the capital, the trails were smoothed out, widened, and covered with mats, the work having been apportioned section by section among the various clans. Thus the bishop never set foot upon the bare ground.

Even more remarkable, the fields, trees, and hillocks along the road were covered with men and women who had flocked to see the bishop. So magnificent was his dress that they thought him a saint sent by God and showered him with gifts—lambs, kids, chickens, partridges, fish—in such abundance that he did not know what to do with them and, like it or not, had to leave them to the poor. Thus the new Christians showed their great zeal and obedience.

Countless men and women, boys, girls, and old people came to meet him, bowed down before him to ask for the water of holy baptism, displaying extraordinary symptoms of true faith and refusing to let him pass until he had met their wish. Hence the bishop was obliged to make many stops, and to carry with him water, salt, and other necessities.

He was led in procession to the church; after he had given thanks to God, he was taken to the home that had been assigned him. He busied himself at once with the organization of the Church and clergy: monks and secular priests.

He raised the Church of Sainte-Croix to the rank of a cathedral; at that time it had eighteen canons and their chaplains, a choirmaster and choristers, an organ, bells, and everything needed for holy worship.

Speeches vibrant with "militant humanitarianism" and the "mission of civilization" were made, and Saif listened impassive, as it was proclaimed that "education will now be compulsory, the colony will be lined with roads, railways, and canals for the greater good of all, in liberty, equality, and fraternity." One had to applaud, and Saif applauded.

On his return home he secretly summoned the native notables to an assembly. The French authorities got wind of it through their agents, but he assured them that his sole purpose was "to communicate the white man's message of peace, happiness, and civilization to the leading black families," and they did not interfere.

This Assembly of Notables, called by the dreaded and magnificent Saif ben Isaac al-Heit, was held on Ash Wednesday, 1902. As custom prescribed, the notables sat cross-legged in the second row, in front of the regional chiefs, behind Saif's counselors, and facing his throne. The emperor, sumptuously attired, was ringed about by his dignitaries, most conspicuous of whom were: his son Madoubo, "a man so strong that with a single stroke of his sword he could split a slave in two or sever the head of a bull"; the Judeo-Negro scholar Moses ben Bez Tubawi, "a doctor extraordinarily versed in the Law, the Koran, the suras, and the Zohar"; the Berbero-Peul copyist Al Hadj Dial; the Sudanese Doumbouya, a wealthy slave trader with the face of a horse, "an authority on the secret slave traffic."

Every word spoken at that memorable assembly smacked of black magic, though here and there lip service was paid to the hypocritical cult of traditional morality.

What, Saif ben Isaac al-Heit asked, should be the attitude of our nobles and notables in the face of recent developments? Understandably, his question was received with hesitation and bewilderment.

And then all hearts were struck with ice. For suddenly the idealist Al Hadj Ali Gakore, a man in his fifties as stooped as a sleeping vulture, was seen to come forward with crisscrossing steps. Tremulous in his ample dashiki, he knelt before Saif, having first sprinkled three pinches of dust on his fine silk-enturbaned headdress in token of obeisance. "If," he began in the caviling tone of a dialectician—"if it is true that the sons of Ham spoken of in the Scriptures are an accursed people, and if we are indeed a part of that black Jewish people descended from the Queen of Sheba, how do you account for our ability to fight against the white man?" Then, strangled by his audacity, his voice quavering at every syllable: "Noble lords, Imam Mahmud, Grand Sherif of Mecca, predicted that after Isaac al-Heit, at the coming of a new caliph, blood and tears would vanish from the world . . . humph, is that true or is it false? That servants and masters, now equal, would devote themselves in common to the service of God, that power would be established in justice and that grandeur would engender itself without cease like . . . the sea. Also that the Empire would be strong and the peoples united, ah yes, by an accumulation of riches, power, and glory which would be . . . hm . . . expended on things pleasing to God, hm. . . ." And crying out as though illuminated: "True or false?"

In conclusion, looking timidly at the imposing Saif ben Isaac al-Heit out of his rheumy eyes:

"Ah, noble caliph! What would men think if you were to forget the ways of educating a people?"

The consequences of his audacity are related by Mahmud Meknud Trare, descended in an unbroken line from griot ancestors and himself a griot in the present-day African Republic of Nakem-Ziuko:

"After that Saif decided that only the sons of the servant class would be constrained to undergo French education, the masses of the missionaries, and the baptism of the White Fathers, to adopt French dress and shave their heads, while their parents would be obliged to make amends and swear secrecy. That the Holy Bibles of the missionaries would be burned as the wind blowing from the Yame fanned the flames which an expert hand would guide to the huts of the Jesuit Fathers. That to incite the notables of the neighboring colonies of the former Nakem Empire to sedition, Tama, a coal-black asp reared in Saif's house—and oh, how poisonous!—would be dispatched at midnight along with three other asps, younger but no less cruel, into the room where the tyrannical governor and his family, as guests of the married and undesirable administrator, were sleeping. And lastly, that for the edification of the masses, Al Hadj Ali Gakore, 'a man of false submission, a hypocrite far too well versed in the art of defamation,' should be subjected to a twofold ordeal—by fire and by poison. He died in the winter of 1902, exploding like an infernal machine a moment after drinking the resinous poison: the flames of the divine judgment set fire to his gaping intestines and he was burned to a crisp." A sob for him.

Who can say how many lives Saif snuffed out? After the auto-da-fé of Al Hadj Ali Gakore, and the "accidental" death of the governor, his wife, the administrator, his wife and daughter, Saif, accompanied by the throng of his dignitaries, appeared before the colonial authorities to lament the dead, deplore their carelessness, and express his regrets at the fires in which six hundred and fifty-three Bibles had been burned.

Saif's appeal, sent secretly to the neighboring colonies, did not fall on deaf ears: certain chiefs imitated him, set fire to the living quarters of the colonial administration, and, to the desolation of the missionaries, burned Bibles and Lives of Jesus by the hundreds. Undesirable colonists and administrators were murdered periodically by the *vipers of the supernatural*. (Other native chiefs, co-operative or cautious or fearful or servile, submitted to the white man in silence.) The next day life went back to normal: wires went out reporting the deaths, requesting replacements, and ordering more Bibles. Since, thought the white man, Africa is and remains the savage continent, what wonder that thoughtless men, suddenly catapulted from the European cradle of civilization into the land of the Blacks, ignoring all advice and letting the grass grow too high around their houses, should fall victim to "poisonous snakes driven out of the woods by fire"? A perfect crime. And as such often repeated. *Mashallah! wa bismillah!* The name of Allah upon us and around us! And forgive us, O Lord.

The next day Saif—*Ya atrash!*—was supposed to marry Tambira and Kassoumi. But having claimed for himself the right of the first night, this being the first marriage to take place among his servants, he pointed out that "the bride must be a virgin." Which was not the case. So the marriage was put off for a month: for after donating a cow, three sheep, four kettles, other kitchenware, and money, Saif sent two old women to establish the bride's nonvirginity.

The matron made Tambira sit with legs spread on a large mortar that had been rolled into her room. And while the first old woman held her motionless, the second, with a knife that was none too clean—*ba'al ma yallah!*—cut off her clitoris, incised the two lips, rubbed them sore, and pinned them together with thorns. Then, making a little opening in this "seam" (for the needs of nature), she inserted a little hollow stick coated with browned butter. After the operation, she covered the woman's abdomen with a triangular bandage of millet straw, extending from her knees to her hips. Tambira was made to lie down on a mat of plaited reeds and forbidden to move until fully healed, nor was she allowed to receive male visitors. The matron prepared her meals and ran the errands.

Saif had meanwhile won the favor of notables and servants alike, and even of the *tirailleurs* and interpreters in the service of the French, by proclaiming a new customary law which made woman irrevocably a man's thing and instrument. To prevent women from being unfaithful to their fiancés, the practice of infibulation (the sewing up of the vagina)—hitherto a rarity— was made the rule; and lest a woman once married should avenge herself by infidelity, her clitoris was removed. This and the fear of the dire punishment for adultery did much to quench the passions of the nigger ladies, who became models of virtue. Men living in concubinage with the weaker sex were delighted with this regulation, for when they married a new sadistic sport, compounded of pleasure and pain, was forced upon them.

Under these conditions an adulteress incurred pitiless punishment: the very least that could happen to her was to be stripped bare, exposed with shackled ankles in the royal courtyard, and given a douche of pepper water to which—*wallahi!*—ants had been added. In certain cases (if the guilty woman was pregnant or had been delivered of a still-born child) another punishment devised by Saif was administered. She "was held with spread legs over a wood fire which singed her pubic hair." On the other hand, a woman whose husband had been unfaithful could do nothing but take note of the fact, seek out her rival, and, having found her—hee-hee-hee!—insult her and thrash her.

After feverish preparations, the long-awaited marriage was held on the first Friday of the following month.

As custom decrees, the slave Kassoumi resorted to magic to secure Tambira's love. Providing himself with a salamander, a cockroach, and an old piece of cloth that Tambira had used to wipe her loins with in the days of their amours, he dried them, ground them up, and mixed them into the tidbits he was to serve his wife after Saif had exercised his right. Then, following the counsels of the old people, he burned nail parings, three eyelashes, seven head hairs, and seven of his pubic hairs, and seasoned the ashes with red pepper: these too he sprinkled on the bride's nuptial viands. To guarantee his own vigor during the seven days of the marriage feast, he crushed three lion penises, the dried sperm of a he-goat, and three cock's testicles into a powder which he mixed with yams and ate with a red sauce.

On the night of this first Friday in March 1902 (the religious ceremony had been performed in the morning by the appointed chiefs), as incense, sublimate of camphor, aloes, Indian musk, and amber were burned in the antechambers, as the women among the guests tinted their hands freshly with henna and their faces with saffron, as the drums, flutes, fifes, cymbals, dulcimers, and xylophones resounded as on great feast days, Tambira, comforted, bathed, and perfumed, received the visit of the matron, who examined her to make sure the stitches were still in place. An hour later Saif, regal magnificence whose every step was said to be an instant of bliss, blasted the barrier of stitches which, luckily for Tambira, had rotted.

To Saif's consternation she showed no pain, but then a trick filled him with delight: the bride, who had slipped a little sack of sheep's blood under her buttocks, contrived to wince; the blood splattered and the sadistic Saif thought he had brought it forth from her entrails. In token of his prowess, the matron displayed a bloody cloth to the guests, and three cannon salutes, barking into the night, were greeted by the songs, cries, roars, and dances of the crowd: *oye oye oye, gouzi-gouzi!*

Then Kassoumi went in to his wife, gave her a symbolic slap in the face, and left the room. This he did three times. Then he brought her food. Late in the night, he consummated the marriage; he would have to perform the act "many times in the six remaining days," so it was said, "to prevent the wound from closing."

In the same month one thousand six hundred and twenty-three marriages were celebrated in the various districts and provinces. The notables had taken the offensive.

The idiot people rejoiced, but in reality the notables were laying the foundations of the future. All these new legitimate couples would soon produce children whom the notables would send to the French mission schools in place of their own. Since the French law must apply to someone, the notables arranged that it should apply to the common people, whom they rounded up and sent to toil for the colonials on roads, railways, and public works. And the white man regarded the notables as his allies! But they whispered to the people: *Azim bouré ké-karato warali:* "The white man has come to enslave you with his forced labor; the sole beneficiary of all these roads and railways is his own colonial commerce." The credulous people became the accomplices of the diabolical notables: in silence and submission they execrated the white men, those demi-gods whom they had formerly worshiped as their saviors.

A number of learned natives whispered very softly what they called "the truth": that Saif was a mere impostor; that there was no more Jewish blood in him than green blood in a nigger. "Why does this miscreant claim to be a Jew? Solely to prove that his ancestry makes him superior to the niggers, whom it is his mission—his as much as the white man's—to civilize. Naturally, niggers can't manage their own affairs or govern themselves. Who ever heard of a black Jew?"

Others insisted that Saif was telling the truth, that he was indeed a black Jew, descended from the Gaonins of Kairouan, from Rabbu Enca Wa of Tlemcen, from Yossef Lackkar, from the Gabilou, from Amram ben Merwas and Jacob Sasportès. . . . As a last resort they brought in the Queen of Sheba. . . . *Allahu Akbar:* let us then pray God for forgiveness. . . .

Two weeks after these events a cable from Paris was received on Mt. Katsena (two miles from the native city of Tillabéri-Bentia): Jean Chevalier, the local subadministrator, was promoted to the rank of administrator and governor ad interim.

Fearing for his life, Chevalier sent for Bouremi, the sorcerer of Krebbi-Katsena, an ambitious man who had betrayed the Gonda and rallied to Saif, betrayed Saif and rallied to the French, betrayed the French and rallied to the Gonda. Then, on the outs with everybody, this impenitent sorcerer and practitioner of occultism had turned professional murderer. Chevalier questioned Bouremi about Saif, his spies and assassins.

Karim Ba the interpreter was a Tukulör slave with six fingers on his left hand. To make a little money he had taken part in various swindles and looting expeditions of the native *tirailleurs.* But as an interpreter he hadn't his equal, being well versed in French, Arabic, and seven of the vernacular languages of Nakem.

CHEVALIER: How many able-bodied men have you got in the village?

BOUREMI: Twenty-eight.

CHEVALIER: What do you mean, twenty-eight?

BOUREMI: I mean twenty-eight, including myself.

CHEVALIER: Dog and son of a dog. You lie. Saif's men told me they had counted three hundred and hadn't yet finished counting.

BOUREMI: I've told you the truth. You can see for yourself.

Saif attacked their canoes and sank them all, there wasn't a single survivor. Just count the widows in the village.

CHEVALIER: Hold your tongue, dog, you're terrified of that accursed Saif [*slaps his face*]. So I'm a liar, am I, I, Administrator Chevalier? I say there are at least three hundred of you. Who do you expect to believe that twenty-eight men would dare to rebel against Saif? His men will cut you into little pieces, little pieces.

BOUREMI: . . .

CHEVALIER: Are you a Moslem?

BOUREMI: No, by the grace of the Most-High and of Mohammed, His prophet.

CHEVALIER: Good. Then you will serve me. You will teach me how to commit murder with poisonous snakes. And I will reward you with gold, women, horses, lands, anything you please.

BOUREMI: Snakes don't commit murder; they only bite people. By accident.

THE INTERPRETER (*to Bouremi*): If I translate your words, your head will fall. . . .

BOUREMI (*to the interpreter*): No matter. I can't tell him the truth. Saif has all the big snake trainers. If the rest of us try to train snakes, the snakes will kill us and the secret will be revealed to all the tribes . . . and to the white men.

CHEVALIER (*irritably*): What does he say?

THE INTERPRETER (*to Bouremi*): May the God of the bush prolong your days . . . (*to Chevalier*): My lord, he says he would like the night to think it over.

CHEVALIER: Very well, take him away. You are responsible for him. But he'd better make up his mind. Or else!

And Bouremi was led away. Karim Ba, the interpreter, showed him his wives, his servants, his horses, and his house, and urged him to obtain like favors by serving Chevalier and, in collaboration with other renegades, setting up a counter-espionage organization. Awake to the danger of his situation, Bouremi hesitated. To rally openly to the French was to condemn his family to occult death at the hands of Saif.

Questioned again, Bouremi repeated that he would give his answer the following day. Then he asked to be taken to a certain clump of ivy, where he wished to gather herbs for a secret decoction. His wish was granted. On leaving the ivy, he asked his guard for permission to satisfy the needs of nature and slipped into a dense thicket beside a stream full of chattering toads. The alarm was given. The beaters came very close to his hiding place, but passed it by. Suddenly the sorcerer felt something sticky licking him, a muzzle, and identified a hyena, no!—two hyenas. He ran out of the thicket screaming. Caught, bound hand and foot, he was taken to Chevalier, who flew into a rage, went through the motions of condemning him to death, and signed him up.

He had acquired a valuable henchman: may he chew the bowels of an ass in the land of the dead!

It was decided that Saif would be assassinated the following month, but by stealth, for any overt action, it was thought, would blow up in his enemies' faces.

But suspicion was aroused by the sorcerer's attempted flight. Saif's agents got wind of it and informed their master, who immediately dispatched a rider to the village chief of Krebbi-Katsena. That same night the village chief sent Awa, a magnificent Peul woman, to Chevalier—who was a widower.

Twice each week the administrator enlisted the services of his interpreter or of the village chief of Krebbi-Katsena to deliver a companion of his lusts to his door. Awa, a fact unknown to Chevalier, was the fiancée of Sankolo, one of Saif's agents. Moreover, she spoke French.

The moment he saw her, the administrator was beguiled by her freshness, by the velvet of her skin, which was amber-colored like that of the Berber nomads. Her eyes had the soft glow of fireflies, her hair was silky, and she had the fine nose of a Tuareg woman. She was dressed in flowered satin in the Egyptian style, with earrings, a necklace of fat pearls, and gold bracelets set with rubies.

Her tresses were of watered silk, her eyes were glowing coals, and in stature and bearing she was unrivaled.

He bade her be seated and rested his hand gently on her knee. A soldier brought in a storm lamp which cast a bar of light across the dark antechamber, and Chevalier, perceiving the woman's expectant smile, withdrew his hand quickly. There must be no unconsidered gestures: it is so easy to create a misunderstanding; with muffled step he preceded her to the veranda which led to the drawing room and the rest of the house.

"I live all alone here," he said sadly and a trifle stiffly. "My wife is dead." (He struck a match, lit an oil lamp, and white walls rose up around them.) "Take an orange while I light the other lamps."

He bent down beside each of the four lamps and the soft flames crackled and purred at the end of his match.

"Not a bad place you've got here," Awa murmured brazenly. "What a lot of books you have."

"Those are the books I have written," the administrator lied.

"It must be wonderful to write."

"One tries to say something. Er . . . would you care to see the rest of the house? It's in excellent taste, don't you think? Of course," and here Chevalier lowered his voice, "it lacks the feminine touch."

The administrator proceeded from room to room, lighting lamps as he went; and in each room there arose, like sentinels at attention: white panels, paintings on glass, cream-colored walls, pale jade-green ceilings. . . .

He never looked around him, sensing the silent admiration of this woman who could not have had better taste: a svelte Louis XVI drawing room, here and there in apparent disorder, attenuating its severity, a rich Persian rug and various objects collected in Indochina and North Africa; in the dining room a Louis XVI silver cabinet and buffet, an alabaster vase, an opaline Buddha, and an Arabian tea set.

The man pursued his round with short steps, calling nothing to Awa's attention, as though wishing to make this woman the humble guardian of his treasures. He inclined his head as though to express his desire to keep this beautiful courtesan for himself and the pride he derived from the perfection of his own taste.

"My bedroom," he said, opening a pink door, standing aside to let her pass, and holding up a lamp.

Awa was breathless with delight at the pink hangings, the semicircular bed, and the silk counterpane which seemed to be strewn with rose petals.

"Oh!" she said, catching sight of a mirror which with its deep reflections flattered her more than the honeyed words of any man. "O-oh," she clucked at the sight of the one picture on the wall. "How pretty she is! Who is it?"

"My wife," said Chevalier, without looking at the picture.

The portrait was straight across from the bed. It was the first face he saw when he woke up. That face bade him good morning, made him a gift of its beauty, its malice, its virtue.

"How you must have loved her!" Awa hazarded, fascinated by the face.

For a moment Chevalier wanted to shout the truth: that his wife was here not because he adored her but because there was no other place for this picture which reminded him of the one being who had seen through him.

He hastened to change the subject. "Come, I'll show you the kitchen."

With its white windows, its white cupboards and tables, its enameled coal stove, and its pastel-blue walls and ceiling, the kitchen seemed to emerge from a dream.

Through the parted curtains Awa saw a magnificent black woman in the house across the way, naked at her mirror, brushing her hair: an enormous double bed awaited her customers. An orderly was setting the table for the next day's breakfast; in another room Captain Vandame was writing while a corporal stood at attention.

"They're all doing something different," she murmured, while her eyes returned to the big bed and her thoughts to the counterpane in Chevalier's bedroom, then to Saif.

Chevalier felt something softly caressing his elbow. Slightly flustered, he turned around, still with his gentle aristocratic smile that could signify almost anything, affected courtesy, for instance, or plain embarrassment. He looked at Awa again, conscious that his elbow was touching her breast and that the woman was *well aware* of it. She made no movement and felt her pointed breast harden against the man's elbow.

Both silent, they looked at the gilt moldings, the zebra skins and paintings on the walls. The air smelled of wild beast and incense; at their feet a panther skin.

The administrator poured champagne. Then in a soft languid voice, confident of the woman's consent:

"To sleep with a black woman," he murmured, turning his feverish eyes upon the bed. "To sleep with a black woman is the pleasure of kings and of the gods of Olympus. It is the greatest of all pleasures, the unavowable delight. Come, little girl, I'll teach you a thing or two."

He stroked the hollow of her belly and kissed her long black neck on either side. Then he left the room and came back with two handsome, powerful setters.

The dogs darted avid glances at them. Their master whistled and Médor, with moist quivering jowls, sprang at Awa.

"Médor," he ordered. "Go to it. It's all yours!"

Before the woman knew what was happening, the setter with his fangs and claws had ripped her clothes to pieces, torn off her loincloth and shift without scratching her skin. Médor must have been uncommonly experienced at that kind of work.

Paralyzed by mingled terror and consent, Awa found herself stripped of her clothes in less than a second. When he saw her naked, Chevalier bent down over her and drew her to a couch of furs covered with a pink silk shawl.

He laid her down and moved his tongue over her copper-red lips, her hair, golden blue like iron, her silver-black eyes, her breasts, warm and soft as two doves of living wool. And suddenly a swelling sigh rose from the woman's lips, brusquely stifled by Chevalier's hand.

Her fingers under her armpits, she arched her back and screamed, feeling against her lips the rasping pungency of Dick's muzzle, while Chevalier grimacing relaxed his caressing of her loins and like a sticky cudgel Médor's hard, pointed tongue explored her vulva.

Maddened by these feverish nibblings, she licked Chevalier's perfumed tongue, struggled and cried out. Calling off the dogs, the man plowed the woman like a fallow field, like an ocean smitten by the prow of a ship. And when he heard her gasping under the emotion of this sin:

"How is my little black girl?" he asked, as torpid as a partridge in the heather. "Have you enjoyed it a little?"

"Oh! I've never seen anything like it," Awa sighed. A slap from him made her bark, she coiled up with pleasure, panting under his cruel caress, manipulating him like a queen or a skillful whore. Her mouth was still hungry for this man's pink, plump mollusk, and the tongue in her mouth itched to suck at the pearl of sumptuous orient that flowed, foaming as though regretfully, from the stem. . . .

The deep peace of pleasure drowned all the fears, all the perplexities of the day; and the woman confessed that she never felt so much at home as in the bed and arms of a man.

A flowing cup—Awa—a lavish board! An Eve with frantic loins, she cajoled the man, kissed him, bit him, scratched him, whipped him, sucked his nose ears throat, armpits navel and member so voluptuously that the administrator, discovering the ardent landscape of this feminine kingdom, kept her there day after day, and, his soul in ecstasy, lived a fanatical, panting, frenzied passion.

A week later Awa unloosed his tongue and sent Saif confirmation of the plot.

"Oh, Saif . . . you know . . . luckily, he hasn't long to live. And the people will thank us." Those were the imprudent Chevalier's exact words.

Once posted, Saif bided his time.

And indeed, three weeks later a letter in Chevalier's hand informed Saif that in consequence of the demise of the governor and of the administrator, he, Chevalier, had been appointed permanent governor, that Captain, now Major, Vandame replaced him as administrator, and that the entire staff had been upgraded. The missive concluded with an invitation to dinner.

At headquarters the whole day was devoted to ceremonies in honor of the promotions, and in the evening Saif arrived, followed by his bodyguard, Hamad, the One-eyed.

An evening in May. The setting sun, which would soon bathe the jagged crest of Mt. Katsena in flames, projected Saif's endless slanting shadow upon the dust-shrouded ocher-colored road. His enturbaned fez was a large dark spot hopping from tree trunk to tree trunk, then falling to the ground and crawling through the underbrush.

A little cloud of impalpable dust rose from beneath his feet and swirled like smoke around his wide gown, while somewhere in the distance a missionary could be heard at prayer: "Come to Jesus. Come to the Lord."

There was dignity and strength in Saif's long, slow strides. Smiling, he caressed the cutlass under his dashiki and, soothed by a light breeze from the plains, sponged his square forehead beneath his graying short-cropped hair—the forehead of a warrior far more than of a religious leader. A few steps from the threshold, he removed his head covering with a somewhat theatrical gesture, revealing an aristocratic, dissolute, and handsome face and the bald crown of his head—a sign of weariness or of early debauchery. His thick lips, his aquiline nose, indeed his every feature smacked unmistakably of vice.

He seized the metal ring and pulled several times. Faint at first, the sound swelled, vibrated, rose to a piercing scream, a hideous plaint of struck copper.

The orderly appeared. His face was tense and he cast fearful angry glances at Saif, as though with his watchdog's instinct he had foreseen the massacre augured by this visit.

The door opened wide and Saif, accompanied by Hamad his bodyguard, made his entrance.

Saif made an impression. Flustered and delighted, Chevalier rushed to meet him.

"But, my dear fellow, it was to be an informal gathering; you see me in my business suit."

"I know," Saif replied. "So you informed me, but I always wear full dress when I go out in the evening."

Holding his enturbaned fez under his arm, he salaamed. A rare object—of massive gold—gleamed in his buttonhole.

Chevalier introduced those present: "Madame Vandame, Major Vandame, the administrator; Madame Mossé, Captain Mossé, their son Jean; Madame Huyghe, Lieutenant Huyghe, their daughter Isabelle, whom we call Isa for short."

Everyone bowed. "Shall we have our apéritifs in the drawing room?" Chevalier asked. And Saif replied: "It is a great kindness."

A servant took Saif's head covering, which he would have preferred to keep, and he looked about for his bodyguard.

They sat down. The others looked at him from afar and no one spoke. "Are your neighbors behaving themselves?" Chevalier asked. "I hate to see them making things so hard for you."

Saif replied in an easy conversational tone: "No. It is all very complicated, we shall have no end of trouble. But with your benevolent assistance all things will be possible."

Chevalier felt obliged to enlighten the ladies. Turning toward them, he explained: "His Majesty helps us to deal with all the knottier native questions. One might say that he in his sphere performs the functions of a governor and an administrator."

The orderly entered, pushing the door with his knee and carrying glasses and bottles on a tray. And Chevalier poured the drinks.

As though by mistake, Saif took Madame Huyghe's glass. She was about to raise Saif's glass to her lips when Chevalier intervened: "You've taken the wrong glass, my dear. . . ."

**59**

Feigning astonishment, Saif turned to the governor, who hastened to explain: "Er . . . Madame Huyghe, I believe, has taken your glass . . . which was full . . . er . . . and liquor doesn't agree with her."

Madame Huyghe was about to contradict him when—*nak gudwa!*—a violent kick in her ankle made her cry out. Her husband made profuse apologies. Saif smiled—there was something smug, almost condescending in his affability—took the glass intended for him, returned the lady's glass, and looked at his bodyguard out of the corner of his eye.

Saif saw in a flash that the others knew nothing. Had she known, would the woman have been prepared to drink? And would they have brought their children with them to witness *that?* No. . . . Chevalier had plotted the whole thing by himself.

"Come," cried the governor. "Dinner is served. You here, Your Majesty, at my right, between Madame Vandame and Madame Mossé, across from Mademoiselle Isabelle. You're not afraid of ladies, I trust."

The dinner began. Saif had drunk nothing. Mindful of his own intentions, Chevalier did his duty as a host, making every effort to sustain a conversation that glided from platitude to platitude; he beamed, joked in a loud voice, was attentive to the ladies, poured champagne: "A bit of this Moët, Your Majesty. I won't call it remarkable, but excellent it is, properly aged and natural, I can guarantee that. You see," he lied, "I have friends in France who send it regularly."

Saif, all smiles, nodded his head, and raised his glass to eye level as though for a toast. A glitter came into his eyes and they narrowed. So that's what the sorcerer Bouremi had concocted: a fine, almost invisible powder of *dabali* mixed with asp venom. The dose was enough to kill him, not on the spot, but next day by a heart attack. The perfect crime.

Putting down his glass and telling some hunting anecdote, Saif scratched discreetly under his left thumbnail and poured the content—more asp venom treated and dried—into his champagne glass.

The meal continued, interminable and magnificent, a true banquet. Dish after dish; champagne and white wine fraternized in neighboring glasses and mingled in the stomachs of the guests. Saif scraped the sauce from each dish with his table knife, so removing the spices that would have made him thirsty, and went on eating and smiling imperturbably. The clinking of the plates, the voices, and the muffled music produced a deep continuous hum, which dispersed into the clear sky—where hovered the notes of the bugle sounding curfew. Fascinated by Saif, Madame Vandame adjusted her bodice over her dancing breasts; the major, flushed with excitement, talked politics while Saif ate but did not drink. Continuing to scrape the surface, he took second helpings of everything, as though he had just noticed that it was wise to feign ignorance, to savor the feeling of his belly filling with good things which have already given pleasure in passing through his mouth. His foot, which he had maneuvered adroitly, was caressing Madame Vandame's foot; nothing was said, but vaguely troubled by his sense of her emotion, he looked at her tenderly, intently, inquiringly, for in that moment he knew that he was slowly, forcefully, serenely raping her.

Then it was time for the toasts. Many were proposed, all worthy of applause. The evening wore on. Already fine milky mists were rising not far off—the airy night garments of peace and the unknown.

A kitten belonging to Chevalier slipped between the feet of the guests. With an intentionally clumsy sweep of his hand Saif upset the poisoned glass that was still before him, but he caught it in time and it did not break; then with a grieved look he gazed at the fatal liquid splattered on the floor. Soon the kitten came and lapped it up.

The conversation, interrupted for a moment, resumed with new animation. But a few minutes later the kitten lay writhing, foaming at the mouth, squealing and miowing, with its four paws in the air. And died.

Saif mimed an outburst of fury. With consummate diplomacy he put the blame on the orderly, who—yes indeed, and he'd better not try to deny it—had wanted to poison him, to kill him, in short to ruin so friendly, so brotherly an evening. . . .

Stunned by this master stroke of horror, Saif's bodyguard had approached his master behind the storm lamp that lit the room, while the orderly, at whom Chevalier was barking furious insults in the presence of his bewildered guests, hastened in stupefied silence to clear away Saif's fork, plates, and knife.

Suddenly Saif decided that the time had come to simulate an assassination plot. As though pushed by the orderly, he jostled his bodyguard, who in falling upset the lamp which exploded and went out. Saif howled as though wounded and at the same time threw something into Chevalier's eye, which it penetrated with a splashing sound punctuated by a cry.

The table was overturned; tumult among the guests. Screams. Moans. For a few seconds the darkness was filled with the bright tinkling of shattered glassware and crockery; then, amidst the gasps of the women and the exclamations of the men, a soft body seemed to be crawling over the floor. Then nothing.

With the breaking of the lamp, night had fallen over them, so sudden, unexpected, and profound that they were stupefied as though by a terrible event. The major ordered everyone to keep calm and not to move. He went out alone. And came back fifteen minutes later with another storm lamp taken from his lodgings some fifty yards away.

The silence and peace of the tomb. Nothing seemed to live or breathe. The moment he opened the door, Vandame shrank back in horror.

Saif was motionless, wedged against the table; Chevalier lay under his chair. And then the others, trembling, their hearts pounding, gasped faintly: "Your Majesty . . . Governor . . ."

No one answered, nothing moved.

"My God, my God," whispered Isabelle. "What have they done? What has happened?"

No one dared to come closer, all were seized with a wild desire to cry out for help, to run away, to scream. They felt their legs giving way under them. The major could only mutter: "Your Majesty . . . Governor . . ."

But suddenly the soldier in him took over; despite his fear, an instinctive urge to help Saif and Chevalier, one of those heroic impulses that sustain fighting men in the field, gave him a terror-stricken courage, and he turned the bodies over. First, all saw Saif stretched out beside the table, asleep or apparently so, then the shattered lamp, then the bodyguard with a wound in the back of his neck, and then, a great tear in the back of Saif's magnificent dashiki. His heart throbbing with fear, his hands trembling, Vandame repeated: "My God, my God, what has happened?"

As he moved forward—very slowly, with little short steps—he slipped on something viscous and almost fell. Bending down, he saw a red liquid on the red floor, spreading around his feet and flowing quickly toward the door. He knew at once that it was blood.

Stricken with madness, Isabelle fled. Throwing away her napkin, she ran from the sight, into the woods in the direction of the village. Followed by her mother, she ran, bumping into trees, screaming, staring at the fires in the distance. Her shrill voice, followed by her mother's screams, cried: "Saif . . . Saif . . . Saif . . ." over and over again.

When she reached the first sentries, frightened men came out with their guns and surrounded her; but she only struggled and did not answer, for she had lost her mind.

In the end they gathered from Madame Huyghe's sobbed explanations that something terrible had happened at the governor's, and a squad ran to his assistance.

Soon lights were flying over the ground, through the trees, between the barracks and administration buildings, in the direction of Chevalier's house. Long yellow swaths traversed the dusty trampled grass, and in the shifting beams the tortured tree trunks coiled and interlaced like snakes. Suddenly the ill-starred house appeared, pink again in the lantern light. A sergeant, two corporals, seven soldiers entered, revolvers in hand.

The door stood open, for a moment they hesitated in fright. Then they went in and saluted the major. Madame Huyghe hadn't exaggerated.

The blood, now clotted, covered the floor like a carpet. It extended to Saif and his bodyguard; one of Saif's legs and the bodyguard's forearm were caked with it. Chevalier lay sleeping, his right eye open, red, hollowed—and on the floor beside him his eyeball, round and purple, a bloody pear, lay spitted on the tip of a table knife.

Saif, too, was asleep—the hypocritical sleep of an assassin. When the soldiers turned him over, he woke up, and so did his bodyguard, who seemed to have been seriously stunned by his fall; the back of his head had hit the lamp. Saif rubbed his eyes in a daze; when he saw Chevalier's body, he seemed suddenly overwhelmed, aghast, and, like his bodyguard, baffled.

Accused of murder and summoned, the orderly, who had been skulking in the vestibule, took to his heels. Someone ordered him to stop. In vain. The next moment a sentry shot him down like a dog. He had paid for his crime.

That was the general opinion. No one suspected that Saif was the murderer or that his bodyguard might have slashed his master's magnificent dashiki by design, to give the impression that the assassin had tried to kill Saif by stabbing him in the back. (May God have mercy on our souls.)

"Your Majesty," wrote Vandame, who had been appointed governor, "I wish to congratulate you with all my heart for the admirable assistance you have given us in this country, and which you gave the late Governor Chevalier, who has been taken from us under such tragic circumstances. Rest assured that I am second to none in admiring the great work to which you have contributed so loyally, at the risk of your life.

"I hope and trust that the minister, to whom I have submitted my report, will reward you as you deserve. I enclose an official citation for distinguished service, which, I am confident, is a mere prelude to the many honors which France will find it a pleasure as well as a duty to confer upon you.

> "Your humble and devoted servant,
> "(Signed) Vandame."

Two months later, on July 14, 1902, Saif was made a chevalier of the Legion of Honor and his sons were invited to pursue their studies in Paris when the time came, as the guests of the French government. (Praised be the Wise, the Knowing One.)

Nine months later Tambira gave birth to quintuplets, who were baptized most Christianly: Raymond Spartacus Kassoumi, Jean Sans-Terre Kassoumi, Anna-Kadidia Kassoumi, René-Descartes Kassoumi, and René-Caillé Kassoumi—at Saif's instigation, the parents and Karim Ba, the interpreter, insisted on these high-sounding names.

In other provinces at the same period, the notables hailed other blessed events—future instruments of their future policies. The Master of the Worlds is powerful, and to Him we must return. Let us then pray to Him for forgiveness. Amen.

### 2

And the tradition relates:

"After the betrothal in the desert Saif required seven centuries of history to the day to forge a core of faithful followers among his people. And the people called Saif 'His Royal Magnificence' and the governor 'His Highness.' And there was rain and there was drought: the first year. *Wakul rabbi zidni ilman!*"

And the tradition relates:

"All of you, baptized in the light of Saif ben Isaac al-Heit, have put on Saif Isaac al-Heit; there is no longer any Black or Jew, you are all one in the glory of His Magnificence."

Thus it was incumbent upon the dynasty to make itself known down through the ages and in every region, in order that all men of good will might have it in their power to become children of Saif. Go, go to him, good people. *Alif minpitjè!* And there was rain and there was drought: the second year.

And the tradition relates:

"Thus Saif ben Isaac al-Heit, descended from the luminous and gentle Saif Isaac al-Heit and scion of Nakem's thirst, had the power to enlighten. And enlighten he did, coming to dwell among us to accomplish, with the help of all, the mission of his heavenly ancestor—to fulfill the wise precept that all men should be saved and united under one leader. *Allah hamdulilai rabbi alamin!*

"And Saif sent the children of the people to the French mission schools and the women to the hospitals, and Saif saw that he was their lord and master."

Saif said: "May the missionaries appease the misery of the humble, may my possessions succor those among you whom I can succor, and may the French law give to the country fruits holding the seeds of order and peace"—and so it came to pass. The country produced natives: the black civil servants thus recruited fed their families according to their deserts, a dialogue sprouted according to the quality of the seed—and Saif saw that Nakem was forging ahead. And there was rain and there was drought: the third year.

Vandame, for his part, brought diplomacy to bear, hung bouquets on door knockers, and inaugurated—*tjok!*—the Secular School for the Sons of Chiefs, which would be compulsory for the sons of the darkie nobles. Taken by surprise like a hyena in a thicket of briars, Saif trembled with indignation, but ably concealed it, as though reassured by the serene secularity of those impenitent apostles of French civilization. A dyed-in-the-wool reactionary, he restricted attendance at this school—secular, to be sure, but alas French—to orphans, noble children born of repudiated mothers, and to the children of families traditionally reputed to be seditious. Damnation! Let the white apes in helmets civilize the pickaninnies, the jigaboos, the niggertrash baboons, all those hopeless idiots who, fishing in the troubled waters of the "cultural mission," knocked themselves out licking the white man's boots and praying to his Christ, sucking the breast and bottle of Abbé Henry's sermons, the spirit of the sons of the Oratory of the Divine Love in Rome, of the Theatine monks, of Angela Merici and her Ursulines, of Theresa of Ávila and the Carmelites, and of all the many others recorded in history who, their faces transfigured with eternal beatitude, had sent human multitudes flocking with howls of joy to the Church.

"Paul, by the will of God apostle of Jesus," sang the niggertrash washed dingy-white by Christian baptism—"he who had been the zealous persecutor of the Christians was transformed by the miracle of Damascus into a still more zealous apostle. And that untiring missionary brought a message of salvation to all men, great and small, rich and poor, men and women without distinction. . . . And one day he saw an amazing thing happen: men came to him from afar, from regions unknown to him, begging him to visit their countries, for many were those who thirsted to hear the word of God. . . ."

Then docile and smiling, the serfs intoned:

"I seek not great designs or splendors that are beyond me, but illumined by my master, I have kept my soul in silence and in peace."

And so carpenters, masons, blacksmiths, weavers, brick makers, peasants, guards, agents, bargemen, errand boys and eunuchs, serfs whose new faith the contemptuous notables regarded with a cold eye, slandering devils moved to tears by the calvary of sweet Jesus the Saviour, cowardly enough to denounce Saif in veiled terms but brave enough to name only his henchmen, caressing and swearing by the Holy Bible, made it known to Abbé Henry that Doumbouya, the Sudanese slave trader, not content to keep slaves for his own use—a social phenomenon observed throughout Nakem—drugged the niggertrash of outlying regions and shipped them to the coast, where he sold them, dazed and defenseless, to Arab traders and "pilgrims" setting out for Mecca. Those who were not sold, the little fishes that slipped through his net, were plied with food containing drugs and aphrodisiacs; so conditioned, they worked without wages, remunerated by a hundred nights of love contributed by prostitutes themselves supersaturated with *dabali,* a passport to color-dreams and unheard-of erotic delights. *Djallè! Djallè! amoul bop! Makoul fallè!*

Evidence piled up to the effect that that same year, shortly before the dry season, Doumbouya had sold six thousand men for shipment to Egypt and Mecca. Obviously he was not alone in this deal; who was behind him? No one was willing to speak like a good Christian; all were stricken with the malefice of silence. Informed by his spies, Saif decided to recall Doumbouya —who was Jesuit and slanderer enough to point a finger at him —to his maker. Wishing to plunge him neatly into the beneficent stillness of eternal sleep, Saif sent his killers, Wampoulo and Kratonga, to Jean Barou the blacksmith.

The agents ordered Barou to kill Doumbouya, the Sudanese slave trader, "by letting his knife slip, as though *by accident,* on his neck."

Barou is all indignation. They offer money. He declines. They become more pressing. Stubborn refusal. Haughty dignity. Does he want to bargain? "No." "Too bad." He stands firm. They remind him that Saif never forgives a rebuff. No answer. However . . . No, he refuses to commit murder. The answer is no. They had singled him out because he hadn't let himself be converted quickly enough, hadn't shown all the zeal expected of a neophyte. He would never call attention to himself again. In the name of his dignity.

"Ha-ha, hee-hee, ha-ha! Kill! Go ahead and kill!" cried the exasperated Wampoulo. "Why shouldn't you kill? Eh? Why not? Just tell me why not? Do it for Saif! A life is nothing. You kill a man because he knows something, because memories go tossing around. Because suddenly, at the fatal moment, he becomes a side of defenseless meat. It's dirty, it stinks, it's in your way, it's loathsome, it's a nuisance. You decide that this rotten carcass isn't your fellow man any more. And suddenly a seething hatred creeps up on you. You kill."

"I kill! . . ."

"You kill!" Kratonga broke in.

"No, really, in my opinion this violence you propose is ridiculous, ridiculous. Look. Tears in my eyes. From laughing." Barou gave the two men a glassy look. "Suppose I did what you're asking. Suppose I knocked off that slave trader before I kick in. Maybe I'd be saving the country. Then you could tell the white men that we niggers are civilized, that the slave trade is a thing of the past. A myth. But to kill. And to love. And to kill again. And to take a rest. And start all over again. Funny way of loving your country. . . ."

"But they'll build a monument to you, Barou, you'll be immortal, in paradise."

"Paradise! Not for me—a dead world. Impressing you with its peace and its instant fulfillment of desires before they've even spoken. It doesn't exist."

"Still, it betokens a better state of being, attractive to those who understand it and discover life in it, the life that is everywhere, a superior life perhaps because it is forever a precious immortal spark."

*Iho yamoun! Eyé yami!*

While feverishly his acolyte poured out this litany, Kratonga unlaced a game bag and pulled out—Heaven preserve us!—the horned head of an asp.

At a sign from its tamer, the asp slides out its full length, then raises its body and lets its tongue flicker malevolently in the direction of Barou. Kratonga crouches with firmly planted legs like a weight lifter, seizes the jet-black cable, and raises it above his head.

But the cry in Barou's throat is stifled, for suddenly the cable uncoils and grips the neck of the terror-stricken blacksmith in a scaly collar. Saif's agents stand at a distance, speaking softly to the snake. During its strange embrace a modulated hiss pours from its forked tongue—a wild, obstinate complaint which streams down over Barou's body. And clinging like glue to Barou's neck, its eyes reduced to tiny slits, the asp hisses, hisses, hisses, while Kratonga, the tamer, commands it, scolds it, speaking more and more quickly, fiercely, piercingly, imperiously: and the murderous beast, slowly relaxing its embrace, slips from the man's neck to his calf, and sinks its fangs into it. Then at last it glides into the half-open game bag and rolls up.

Kratonga has closed the game bag; Wampoulo gives Barou to understand that he can now decide whether he prefers to live and kill Doumbouya, or to refuse and die because he has heard too much.

And the tamer adds with irony: "We have our whole lifetime to be unhappy in. Remember the fairy tale: Destiny had an appointment with God in the Land of Love. On the way, he saw some men fighting in an open field. He tried to reconcile them, but in vain. Exasperated, he said to them: 'There is no justice without love, or injustice without necessity.' And in the name of necessity, Destiny massacred the men. Brandishing the torch of reason and leaving it to the survivors—whom he blessed—he went flying on his way and arrived at the meeting place. Too late. God was absent. The torch in the hands of the men behind him was extinguished. God had chosen. So had Destiny. So had man. Do you understand, Barou?"

"What do you want of me?" the blacksmith stammered feebly.

"Doumbouya's life."

Barou nodded his head in submission. Jeering at his look of terror, Wampoulo and Kratonga approached him, dagger in hand: They were going to murder him. . . . But the snake tamer:

"Sorry, I'll have to bleed you. Just a scratch."

First he made an incision at the point where the fangs had entered the calf, then he scarified the blacksmith's skull at the fontanel. Over both wounds he strewed a medicinal powder and put a pinch of it in Barou's nostrils as well. It soon induced sneezing and drew purple blood from the blacksmith's body, which was little by little drained of the venom. Unresisting, he sank into a stupor, a terrified ecstasy, troubled only by his strangled, stertorous breathing.

"I'm losing my blood," he whispered, his mind sunk in the black mire of pain.

"Aha, the blacksmith needs blood! That ought to make him a splendid murderer."

"I'll do it as soon as I can."

"Sure?"

"Yes, masters."

"Sit down."

"Yes, masters."

"We want to talk with you."

"Yes, masters."

"It's essential."

"Yes, masters."

And so it came to pass.

Doumbouya gave Barou his head to shave and his neck as well, and the blacksmith's trembling knife dug into it, severing the life thread of this man who "himself murdered more than six hundred slaves" in the golden age when that sordid trade authorized every crime. A salver of incense for the departed slave trader.

And now the master stroke of horror: To "thank" Barou, Saif sent him a cartridge belt, bidding him adjust the straps.

One of the sons of Kassoumi and Tambira, Raymond-Spartacus Kassoumi, then aged five, brought it to the blacksmith in his shop. Wampoulo, dispatched a few minutes later to call for Raymond and go through the motions of paying Barou his blood money, secretly dropped a cartridge in the hot coals where the bellows rested, and left the smithy, taking the child with him.

Before they had even reached the palace, barely two hundred paces from the smithy, an explosion shattered the bellows, and stove in Barou's chest, killing him instantly. A tear for him.

The same day Abbé Henry called on Saif, who was "ill" and could not see him. He came back the next day and the next—

and was not received until the fifteenth day after these events, by which time it was generally agreed that the cartridge missing from the cartridge belt, the leather of which was very slack, had been fatal to the blacksmith, "a careless man, but esteemed by all, from Saif down." The Abbé's chief witness was dead, his evidence was gone. Not a trace of the gold sent as pay for the crime; Wampoulo had picked it up on his way out.

As though to tell the Abbé to mind his own business, the wily Saif, after reminding him of the theological foundation of the missions, pointed out that the mystery of Israel resides in its refusal to accept the Gospel. "But," he said, "I wouldn't pass judgment if I were you. For the Church with its hierarchy and its credo might well be charged with hypocrisy: 'The first will be last.' "

After a brief reference to his Jewish ancestry, Saif spoke the insidious words: "Israel is here to admonish the Church to vigilance. . . ."

Then, once he was sure the Abbé had caught his meaning, he covered up his tracks by embroidering on his idea.

"Vigilance in regard to the need for individual conversion: It is a mistake," he said heatedly, "to speak of a collective rejection. A collective rejection of Jesus Christ is no more thinkable than a collective profession. It is essentially the concern of the individual. Let us be on our guard against speaking of Israel's rejection or Israel's conversion; these are hasty if not erroneous generalizations.

"Vigilance, too, is needed lest the Church regard itself as an end.

"And lastly, vigilance toward the idea of the 'remnant.' It might suggest that man's fidelity plays a part in the coming of the kingdom of God. No, God acts alone in His grace. But this 'remnant,' present in the Old Testament, recurs in the New Testament and in the Church. It is a bond between the Old Testament and the New, it marks their unity and is the unifying bond between the pre-Christian Church and the post-Christian Church."

And Saif concluded: "Missionary activity among the people

of Nakem—fetishist, Moslem, and black Jewish—confronts the Church with the question—a question that has lost none of its timeliness—of its justification and existence." *Alif lam!*

### 3

The confused relations between the Church mission and the native authority were fraught with consequence. 1909 was the decisive year.

This is what happened:

"Be it known by these presents, given by order and authority of the most-mighty and most pious Saif ben Isaac al-Heit, King by his holy grace, that on the tenth day of April of the present year one thousand nine hundred and nine, in this city of Tillabéri-Bentia and in the palace of His Royal Magnificence, His aforesaid Magnificence gave order that in the presence of myself, the undersigned registrar, the present document be transmitted to Governor Vandame, military prosecutor and principal of the local school, with a transcript of the inquiry that has been made into the treason plotted against His Magnificence by Bishop Thomas de Saignac. It being the desire of His Royal Magnificence that his brother, the white governor of Nakem, be apprised of the truth, he has ordered the issuance of the present document.

"I, Karim Ba, public scrivener and interpreter to Our Highness the Governor; more recently appointed registrar to His Royal Magnificence Saif ben Isaac al-Heit, have transcribed the following word for word:

"Transcript addressed by His Royal Magnificence to M. Vandame, prosecutor and governor, of the inquiry into the machinations of Bishop Thomas de Saignac against His Royal Magnificence.

"On the tenth day of June of the year one thousand nine hundred and eight, in the city of Tillabéri-Bentia and in the palace of His Royal Magnificence. In the presence of the college of native notables and of myself, the aforesaid registrar, His Royal Magnificence gave order that certain witnesses be questioned and that an inquiry be made into the manner in which Bishop Thomas de Saignac has circumvented the pact concluded between the government in the person of Our Highness and His Royal Magnificence by attempting to have this latter kidnaped and to seize his rich lands for the benefit of his diocese and parishes, and at the same time to convert the common people in their entirety to Christianity.

"His Royal Magnificence Saif ben Isaac al-Heit ordered me, Karim Ba, Registrar, to draw up this document and to question all the witnesses summoned by His Royal Magnificence—all of which has been done.

"And I wrote as follows:

"Item. Kassoumi, servant to His Magnificence, married and father of five children. Having duly sworn with his right hand on the Holy Scriptures presented to him by the learned Moses ben Bez Tubawi, the witness testifies that he saw the sorcerer Bouremi and Bishop Thomas de Saignac conversing together on several occasions. The witness further declares that to the best of his knowledge they were closely acquainted and on terms of great friendship, since they conversed only when alone. He adds, however, that he knows nothing more. Nevertheless the witness declares under oath that he saw Al Hadj Hassan, the Grand Marabout, enter the church and speak with Bishop Thomas de Saignac: the entire interview, the witness testifies, took place in the sacristy behind closed doors. However, the witness declares once again, he did not know what they were talking about. Deposition signed in my presence and registered by me, Karim Ba, interpreter and registrar.

"Item. Moses ben Bez Tubawi. Having sworn by the Scriptures, the witness testifies that the aforementioned bishop called out to him one day when he, the witness, was passing within arrow flight of the church. The bishop told him, the witness, that he wished to speak to him in private. He then asked Moses ben Bez Tubawi, a scholar of high repute, to take oath, for he wished, so he said, to confide in him a great secret. The witness claims that he declined to swear and argued the point stubbornly, assuring Bishop Thomas de Saignac that he could speak freely and that he (Moses ben Bez Tubawi) would divulge nothing of what he (the bishop) would say.

"The aforesaid Bishop de Saignac asked him again to take oath, whereupon the witness swore to say nothing. The bishop then confided in a whisper that he had decided, with the understanding of the government authorities, to kidnap His Royal Magnificence Saif ben Isaac al-Heit on the pretext of sending him on a visit to Europe in the company of his son who was going to study in France. Bishop de Saignac told the witness Moses ben Bez Tubawi that he should not fear to accompany His Royal Magnificence—or at least pretend to accompany him —in order to allay his suspicions; and that most of the faithful followers of His Royal Magnificence would go with him. These last of course would be duly brought back. The witness denies having made any reply whatsoever to Bishop Thomas de Saignac.

"When the aforesaid bishop saw that the witness made no reply, he offered him gold, which the witness refused. Then he sent for Al Hadj Hassan and the sorcerer Bouremi, and bade them put pressure on the witness. But the witness declares that he declined to have anything to do with it and left the church. On the morning of the following day, the aforesaid Bishop de Saignac sent for them, the aforesaid witness and the Marabout Al Hadj Hassan, and read them a communication to the effect that the President of the French Republic ordered Saif ben Isaac al-Heit to betake himself to the Atlantic coast, whence he would board ship for Europe and France. This communication could only have been hypocrisy and the use of forgery with intent to get rid of His Royal Magnificence and to confiscate all or a part of his lands for the benefit of the Church.

"Item. Four years previous, on the occasion of the first Christian baptism performed by the missionaries in Nakem, on Easter Sunday April third of the year one thousand nine hundred and five, in the presence of more than eight hundred men, domestics and former vassals of His Royal Magnificence Saif ben Isaac al-Heit, His Royal Magnificence sent them his blessings, accompanied as custom decrees by a donation in evidence of his good will: a strip of land eighteen leagues in length bordering his fields and four leagues in length bordering his orchards. Disregarding this mark of co-operation on the part of His Royal Magnificence, Bishop de Saignac had the audacity to do what certain white traders had advised: to seize all the idols belonging to the converts and order a solemn rite. But only the more recent and inexpressive of these mask-idols were burned. And certain soldiers—former servants of His Magnificence, recruited in 1906 by Mangin, colonel of infantry and cavalry who marched them all the way to Morocco—were surprised on their return to France to see that those same masks, those same idols, far from having been burned as Bishop de Saignac alleged, had been sold at exorbitant prices to antique dealers, collectors, museums, and shops. The profits went to the Church, which claimed to have been ruined in Nakem by the afflux of the needy, their dire poverty, and the inadequacy of the Church subsidies.

"Item. A number of the agents of His Royal Magnificence report that Bishop de Saignac accused His Royal Magnificence of encouraging the common people to flock to the Church for the sole purpose of creating insuperable financial difficulties for the Church and so insidiously casting discredit upon it. This slanderous allegation is in no wise justified by the attitude of His Royal Magnificence. On the contrary, His Royal Magnificence attached so much importance to the mission of the Church that, observing that certain of his servants mocked and insulted the new converts, ceased to respect them and even pursued them, creating a tumult at the very doors of the church, he would have killed them had he not been deterred by his respect for Your Majesty and by his unwillingness to provoke dissension among the people, for some of the guilty parties were among the country's leading citizens.

"Item. Nevertheless, after the failure of Bishop de Saignac's plot, His Magnificence, who had been traveling in Gagol-Gosso, returned at the end of two weeks to find that fifteen of his children, all aged eight, had been poisoned and were dying of dysentery. The sorcerer Bouremi was named; and while they were looking for proofs the sixteenth child of His Magnificence (Hassim, likewise aged eight), having slept one night on one of the palace terraces, broke out shortly afterward with festering pustules: yaws—because an evil liquid had been sprinkled on his body during his sleep. A high fever, added to the extreme exhaustion provoked by his endeavors to save his soul for the Lord, caused his blood, after two daybreaks of agony, to freeze in his veins; and death, which none could avert, crushed his heart in its hands after making him suffer bitterly. Blood spurted from his nose and mouth. One whom death attacks so cruelly cannot resist it. So that this blessed son gave up his soul to the Creator, to be rewarded for the glorious sufferings he had endured for Him. Mournful vigil was held for him—great loss and great sorrow for all those who loved him and were with him.

"And that was not all. At dusk on the third day, Prince Madoubo, eldest son of His Royal Magnificence, who was the guest of France eight years ago, felt suddenly indisposed; his heart beat very fast; his body became burning hot; his blood curdled; he changed color; he turned black, then blue, then pale; and soon he was covered with the fatal pustules that had just carried off his young brother. Appearing before the king that same morning in the courtyard of the palace, he spoke frankly to those assembled there: 'I know well that many people do not love me as Death loves me, as my father loves me. Only eight years ago you solemnly recognized me as prince; my father honored me with this title and later on you found me worthy of its glory. You and my father promised me the kingship, though I never asked for it. Since you want to take it away from me now and send me to my death, you can do so, I will content myself with God and my right.'

"This brief harangue so moved and confounded the Court that the source of the prince's illness was not long in taking on the names of the sorcerer Bouremi (but there was no tangible proof) and of Bishop de Saignac already accused of so many crimes, not to mention the accusation, raised by the families in question, that he got three black women with child.

"Your Highness, you see what things have been going on here, the proofs of these things are innumerable, and no patience can endure them. We tell you no more than what is true—and the truth is that the Fathers of the Society of Jesus who were sent here are certainly virtuous and set a good example. If they have not been respected as much at the end as at the beginning, it is because they coveted the lands of His Magnificence, because they plotted against him, meddling in the political life of the natives, stealing masks and the old doors of the most artistically decorated huts, and this without scruple.

"Moreover, Bishop de Saignac has slandered the notables of His Magnificence from the pulpit, calling them exploiters, slavers, and ignoramuses, and after coming down from the pulpit he said: 'Thus far I have spoken, yes, but not enough of the Jew Saif ben al-Heit; now I am speaking of him and will have more to say.' This he said on the last step, wearing his biretta. All were indignant at hearing His Royal Magnificence thus named. It is recommended that Your Highness hear the sworn testimony of the aforesaid Kassoumi: he is an honest man and cannot deny the truth.

"That is the main reason for the displeasure of His Magnificence, of the notables, and of a large part of the people, to wit, that such public disrespect has been shown His Royal Magnificence: for God does not suffer infidels or Jews to be defamed, witness the case of Elijah: because he permitted his children to dishonor the tribes of Israel, God granted that he die suddenly and that his sons perish by the sword and his daughters-in-law in childbed. Nor should Your Highness countenance such a thing. And that same ecclesiastic also said to us from the pulpit that he wished it might please God to kill him in that very place, and that he regretted only one thing, that we did not do so.

"Furthermore, the aforesaid Bishop de Saignac, while in Goro Foto Zinko, spoke to the commandant and urged the ecclesiastics not to come here. And indeed some were most grieved not to come. Therefore Your Highness ought to ask him for the letters he wrote from Goro Foto Zinko, and have him questioned concerning his intentions and his motives, and Your Highness will see that it is as we say.

"Item. A friend of Kassoumi, converted to Christianity, one Jean-Pierre Dogo, said to Bishop de Saignac: 'Monseigneur, you must procure money. Sixteen of the children of His Magnificence have died and the eldest is seriously ill; it is right and proper that a man of his power receive so many gifts that all his subjects can carry something away. At present he needs but one thing, your support, your help. It is fitting that he should obtain it.'

"Bishop de Saignac replied without hesitation: 'Dogo, I haven't got a single one of his centimes.' Dogo didn't beat about the bush. 'Monseigneur,' he said, 'if you have none of his, you have plenty of your own, your profits from the land he was generous enough to make over to you; he has never ceased to ply you with riches and favors.'—'Dogo, it's no use; I have no riches of mine or of his that I can remember; I'm not a banker, you know; that's the long and short of it.'

"And so it came to pass that the man who had owned everything was short of money; despite the private assistance of Your Highness, your wife, your white subordinates, the needs of His Royal Magnificence could not be met, and still Bishop Thomas de Saignac would not listen to reason; and the poor who had flocked from all sides, to the number of at least forty thousand six hundred, to offer their condolences, were made to wait in vain. They had been deceived by custom; for at the death of members of the royal family it is the custom to distribute generous alms.

"We pray Your Highness to send someone who will inform you of the truth. May co-operation, life, and the royal rank of His Magnificence, his friendship for Your Highness and France, may the Greatness of the Most-High, in His benevolent Mercy, keep you forever in their holy charge.

"In this city of Tillabéri-Bentia, on the tenth day of April of the year one thousand nine hundred nine.

"King Saif ben Isaac al-Heit."

Vandame sent Saif medicines which reached Tillabéri-Bentia that same week, in time to save Madoubo, just as it became known that Bishop de Saignac had left the country, that Saif had been granted a monthly subsidy in addition to a private gift from Monsieur and Madame Vandame, and that the sorcerer Bouremi had gone mad.

Doubts arose as to his innocence. Each day brought new confirmation of the rumor that he had plotted a heinous crime against the person of Saif (who, it was said, had punished him for it). Saif's popularity rose higher than ever, while Bouremi flung himself into wild debauchery.

Not that he raped anyone or got drunk; no, the talk was more of degrading indiscretions, not to say misconduct, acts of violence, of gratuitous sadism, of savagery: he was said to have poisoned private wells; to have infected neighbors with dread diseases by means of elixirs compounded of human blood and leper's pus; to have distilled potions that sowed hysterics far and wide; committed ordalic murder, propagated yaws and the terrible black plague; and lastly married a lady, with whom he once had a riotous affair, to a notable, then made her epileptic and driven her to suicide.

He went about like a swashbuckling rebel, slandering Saif, picking fights with all and sundry, yielding to every caprice; he was in love with his attacks of madness and with their constancy, dreading any change in them, and insulting people for the mere pleasure of it.

Those who thought they knew him regarded him as an idealist, illumined for brief moments by some immense idea which left him dazed, sometimes for too long. He was powerless, so they said, to dominate his idea, he believed in it so firmly, so passionately that his whole existence became a slow agony under its crushing weight. A rebel? A cynic? A scoundrel? The living myth of a personified rage, at the mercy of his neurotic legend? A sorcerer gone wrong? No. Not exclusively, other epithet was found for him: a retired criminal.

Only a week before, to be sure, his wife had decided to go to Saif, to confess and beg forgiveness; on the point of leaving the house, she fell sick. And died. He for his part, abandoning his second wife, who attended to the burial of his first, went right on proclaiming that Saif was engaged in the slave trade, that he had had him, Bouremi, drugged by his agents, his horde of poisoners, to avenge himself, to make him mad, to kill him slowly, to murder him! Because Saif wanted to be the strong man, on the side of the Whites. And Bouremi went about shouting these words, bellowing them, singing them in the streets, stopping the passers-by, peering at them out of his colorless eyes, as though his distrust of law, order, people, the conformist world never left him a second's peace. "The world and its stupidity, I'll wager! If you want to reason with that animal, you'll have to tie him first! A simulator! A madman whom wickedness has haunted so long that it has settled down inside him," scoffed a partisan of Saif, nauseated by the sight of Bouremi, by the look in his eyes, as inexpressive as a half-open oyster. Bouremi couldn't care less; all that, he croaked, was "extraneous," he had ears only for "his truth," to wit, that "Saif is an incendiary blackguard, a slave trader, a false chief, a false Black, and a false Jew, who had murdered Chevalier and oh, how many more! . . ."

"When my madness sets in," cried Bouremi, "I cease to be a man, I become an imaginary being. The devil's being is nonbeing. If he existed, he'd only be a poor devil. . . . What makes a man diabolical is that he has lost his soul. You watch for the tragic event, you feel it coming, but it is never present. That's how it is with Saif.

"The sense of the tragic is devoid of foresight. As you feel the tragedy coming, it happens before you know it, with infinite speed. . . .

"I regard myself as mad. It's true, I was born in the middle of a cemetery and at my birth a thousand stars spurted from my nostrils, splattering, tearing the night with sparks. . . . I . . . aaah, Saif! . . . I'm cold, I'm trembling, my teeth are chattering. . . . No, not even that. I've lost all my teeth in the long fight with life that has laid me low, and I regale the air with the idiotic laugh of my gums undermined by the caries of twenty centuries of history. I've been wanting to speak for a long time, the wars, the ruptures, the treaties, the political tensions between countries held me back, but today I speak and silence is amazed that after so many centuries of galloping inhumanity I have managed to preserve some hope. . . . But, on the other hand, who will tell these silences, these men, these creatures, this whole existence which envelops me and from which I shall tear myself free! who will tell these threepenny fag ends of humanity that I speak to show where I stand or perhaps only for the sake of speaking, because in the long run silence is unbearable. . . . No one here perceives Saif in my words, but when you have all learned how to see, the echo of the ocean within you with its stormy yet weary waves, running down your cheeks in streams of liquid jewels, will gush from your unwashed eyes and you will weep—will weep, my brothers. But enough.

"Open!

"Open, I say!

"My eyes are open!

"A burden on my neck . . . I don't know if you've understood me, but madness is a fine thing, a marvelous alibi, sweet and terrible, you play, you *know* what's what, and suddenly you howl! I've a right to go mad, who's going to stop me? I have neither father nor mother nor God nor Devil. Against Saif I choose madness, others call it a way of being interesting, original, but what if my personal originality is madness? Well?"

And the sorcerer bleated words of philosophy about the misery of the human condition, hailed passers-by, begged for alms, implored people to listen to him, his voice bristling with rage and his lips clogged with terrible words, spewing and spluttering that he was sick of being sullied with slanders, that he had "indeed killed more than a hundred and twenty innocent people," but "by accident." Something in him revolted him, gripped him, tortured him, made him scratch and curse and howl and flail about, and rave that it had been by accident. Accident. Accident. Accid . . . Why didn't they leave him alone? In peace! All he wanted was peace. . . . All by accident! he bellowed, his face ashen, drawn, terrified. Saif? His children . . . Their death? He still had his wits about him. . . . But if, having spoken the whole truth, he was agitated, pacing this way and that, retracing his steps, suddenly resuming that furtive gait, it was because the place horrified him, filled him with terror. He screamed, he wanted to end it all, but out of a kind of devilry, yes devilry, he came back haggard and trembling to castigate Saif's villainy. What's that? The governor knows the truth! They had no proofs. The witnesses were questioned. He hadn't tried to kill Saif. He was innocent! . . . He proclaimed his innocence! Saif had suddenly overturned the glass . . . and the cat . . . and maybe the children died because the cat drank, or a moment of inattention . . . They had no proof! He was innocent! They had heard the plaints of the mourners, the wailing women, rising from Saif's bereaved palace, and that was all! But they should leave him in peace! Accidents happen. . . .

"Accidents?"

"Or strokes of fate! Wait! Listen to me! Something I've got to tell you! Let me explain. . . ."

But Bouremi explained nothing at all, because everyone ran away. Even so, a new trend of opinion set in. The French authorities and a part of the native public were troubled by Bouremi's ravings, which, so it seemed, were not all unfounded. No, perhaps not. But then the sorcerer did something that destroyed his newly acquired credit and caused him to be execrated by all.

Frothing with anger and exhaustion, Bouremi returned home to Bintou, his second wife. The look on his face must have been frightful, for when Bintou asked him to pull himself together in honor of the child, he yelped:

"What?"

"Your child!"

"Who? Who? Me? Me?"

"You."

"Me?"

"It's our child, thanks be to Heaven . . . our child," she repeated, touching her belly with a feverish, cautious palm laid flat. "He's alive, my darling; he's alive, Bouremi, I feel him in there, moving, our . . . our baby, Bouremi. . . . Our baby . . . respect him . . . The neighbors . . ."

"What? . . . What? A baby! You're pregnant by that viper? Ha-ha, so that's why you've been all bloated lately, why you've been wearing those baggy clothes! And me thinking it was just some whim or maybe you were getting fat! You wanted to hide it, eh? That brat! That bastard!"

"Bouremi! No, no! Don't do that! Not that! Bouremi! Bouremi! Bouremi! No! Aaah . . ."

One, two, three, seven kicks in the belly. Seven kicks the brute gave her! Head on! Too few, he said. He'd have given her a hundred. Free of charge. But already she lay still and would have died if the neighbors hadn't held her husband. Anger flared around the sorcerer's hut; roused in a twinkling, the whole neighborhood reviled Bouremi, grabbed him, lifted him above the crowd, tossed him in the air—and let him crash to the ground like a sack of soft dough. They did it three times over, but then, suddenly coming to life, he stamped his feet, gagging on the curses that rose to his throat, threatening to kill them all, took to his heels, pursued by his tormentors; and, this time genuinely mad, threw himself in the Yame River. A cry, shouts from the bank, the rise and fall of horror crushed the crowd, for three crocodiles seized him, cut him in two with a snap of their powerful tails, and tore him to pieces.

The next day Bouremi's wife died in childbed, giving birth to a premature child who weighed only two pounds and was baptized David Bouremi. Magnanimous and politic, Saif adopted him. A hymn for him. *Al hamdulilai rabbi alamin.*

4

A year and three months later—July 13, 1910. Three foreigners, a family of Germans—Fritz Shrobenius, his wife Hildegard, and their daughter Sonia—who had arrived in Nakem five days before, left Vandame in Krebbi-Katsena and, rifles slung from their shoulders, drove to Tillabéri-Bentia in a truck chock-full of trunks, crates, baggy trousers, short-sleeve shirts, and tropical helmets.

Informed first by his agents, then by government emissaries, that these tourist explorers were anthropologists wishing to buy three tons of old wood regardless of the cost and a carload of native masks, Saif ordered a sumptuous welcome.

He sent the learned Moses ben Bez Tubawi, mounted and accompanied by a large retinue, to meet them outside Tillabéri-Bentia. At a league from the city three native delegations, followed by a large body of griots and domestics, approached the visitors, who had slowed their truck to a crawl.

Magnificent, they advanced in groups caparisoned in gold, leather, and brass, amidst a tumult of drums, horns, and other sonorous instruments, prancing in single file in a manner recalling the processions of olden days in celebration of victories in battle. Three or four groups on foot chanted verses from the Koran, and the massed chorus gave the responses. From time to time a cry rose from the entire crowd, piercing the air and seeming to fill it with litanies in praise of the governor, of His Royal Magnificence, Saif ben Isaac al-Heit, and of the German visitors, "for the exploits with which they have honored Nakem."

All Saif's men returned to the palace in the order in which they had left.

Arrived at the palace, Fritz, Hildegard, and Sonia descended from the truck and went to meet Saif, who was awaiting them in the great Courtyard of the Acacias. The crowd was so dense that they had a hard time making their way through it.

Beside his son Madoubo on a high dais sat Saif enthroned—he could be seen from far off. His throne, of gold, ivory, and wood skillfully carved in the manner of the country, harmonized with his magnificent dashiki of ocher velvet, veined with strips of silver through which his damask blouse could be glimpsed. On his head a crown of finely chiseled gold; nonchalantly both he and his son waved Oriental fans, mounted with mother-of-pearl. Moorish pantaloons and babouches completed Saif's accouterment.

Stepping before Saif, Shrobenius made a low bow, and his wife and daughter did the like; the royal personages returned their greeting and in token of welcome presented them with the traditional sip of water. Then the visitors were bidden to be seated.

These courtesies completed, the anthropologist, in the presence of the attentive populace, set forth—with Karim Ba as his interpreter—the purpose of his visit. He opened the door of the truck and a domestic unloaded various pieces of cloth, in addition to which the anthropologist displayed, with all due reverence and respect, silver coins, garments, and jewels. With a magnificent gesture Saif ordered that this inventory should cease and bade the learned Moses ben Bez Tubawi distribute these treasures among the people. And the crowd on their knees kissed the ground in a frenzy of faithful gratitude, while prayers poured from their lips, a quivering litany of words which died down, then revived from time to time like the flame of an almost extinguished fire.

Later on, Saif, whose popularity had risen to new heights, took the German to a place removed from the niggertrash, where, in the presence only of his wives and of his most esteemed courtiers he examined the remaining gifts—but this time very slowly.

After displaying numerous offerings intended for the notables' wives, Shrobenius presented His Royal Magnificence with five pounds of gold bullion. The bargain was concluded.

Next day the anthropologist began taking down the words of informants sent by Saif; his wife tripped up and down the corridors, harassing Karim Ba with interminable questions. Or strolled about between her daughter and Madoubo, who spoke indefatigably of symbols, as did his father, who spouted myths for a whole week. "The night of the Nakem civilization and of African history," droned the prince, "was brought on by a fatal wind sprung from the will of the Most-High."

Saif nodded gravely. Shrobenius's head teemed with ideas. Reeling off spirituality by the yard, the men paced the courtyard with anxious, knit brows. The lean, long-legged Hildegard tagged after her husband, a large stout man, the type of the *bel Allemand,* red side whiskers, florid complexion, blue eyes, grave and full of feeling, nascent paunch, *wèrèguè wèrèguè!*

Saif made up stories and the interpreter translated, Madoubo repeated in French, refining on the subtleties to the delight of Shrobenius, that human crayfish afflicted with a groping mania for resuscitating an African universe—cultural autonomy, he called it—which had lost all living reality; dressed with the flashy elegance of a colonial on holiday, a great laugher, he was determined to find metaphysical meaning in everything, even in the shape of the palaver tree under which the notables met to chat. Gesticulating at every word, he displayed his love of Africa and his tempestuous knowledge with the assurance of a high school student who had slipped through his final examinations by the skin of his teeth. African life, he held, was pure art, intense religious symbolism, and a civilization once grandiose—but alas a victim of the white man's vicissitudes. Then, obliged to acknowledge the spiritual aridity of certain manifestations of social life, he fell into a somnolent stupor, no longer capable even of sadness. Having run out of inspiration, he consoled himself by driving down to the Yame in the truck and filming the hippopotamuses and crocodiles. There, during the hot siesta hours, he would lie in wait, soon relieved by his daughter, an opulently beautiful blonde of twenty with flashing teeth, who would take his place amid the tall grass and the foliage. With her exquisite freshness, her long white neck, her green almond-shaped eyes, her blue lashes tinted with mascara, her pink, firm lips, she made one think of the delicately colored nacreous scales of the fish that furrowed the unknown depths of the Yame.

Madoubo often came to keep her company. He would stand

leaning against the truck, listening to the slow music of her phonograph or explaining in a murmur why Zobo Island in the
Yame was interesting for its pieces of ancient art, how these
pieces had been preserved, and roughly from what periods they
dated. And he invented as vividly as if he had been there in
person.

Sonia had such a delightful way of putting him at his ease, of
throwing herself into her work, of taking notes with a view to
interpreting his meaning and making herself understood, of smiling, of saying *ja* or *nein* in between her sentences sprinkled with
Germanisms, that Madoubo could have stayed there forever, listening to her and looking at her.

One day when they were strolling at some distance from the
palace, followed unbeknownst to them by Sankolo, she suddenly
murmured: "You are very nice."

Her large eyes shone like two muted lamps; her lips were
parted in a luminous smile, and Saif's son was goaded by desire.

Walking slowly, they headed for the shady banks of the
Yame, and soon they discerned the faint, strange, continuous
roar of a wave racing with prodigious speed toward the shore—
gliding, miaowing, rising, yelping, and spreading out like an enormous stain.

They stayed there a long while chatting, hand in hand, peering
between the dead tree trunks cast up by the Yame at the yellow
river, which churned and whirled and bubbled, and played over
the flotsam at the edge of the water, where a family of hippopotamuses were tumbling drunkenly.

Sonia had nestled against Madoubo's shoulder—and the silence was as sweet to them as a kiss.

The appeal of the exotic? of youth? of pleasure? In their lan-
gorous fever, they neither knew nor understood; they kissed
each other full in the mouth and their hard teeth had the savor
of sweet seaweed. . . .

They said nothing but stood face to face, looking down with
perplexed eyes as though lost in a difficult meditation, sensing

something new in the air, breathing the invisible—a mysterious message that told them of their secret intentions, paralyzing them with quivering passion—caught in that sudden tension which extends to the fingertips, which arouses every faculty of physical sensation to the bursting point and culminates in the ineffable need to do something foolish.

Finally, unable to endure it any longer, the two young people set out in search of a safe, secluded place.

Sonia took the lead, running toward the bank of the Yame.

"Is it still far?" Madoubo asked.

"The truck, down there."

"That won't do."

"Oh, you'll see, it's very big. I was lying in there only yesterday, filming the hippopotamuses."

She opened the door quickly and climbed up on the back seat, jostling various objects. Her voice called gently from within:

"Come on."

Madoubo looked around and did not see Sankolo, who had thrown himself down in the rushes. He got in, resolutely setting his hands on her blouse; her lips opened under his.

"Just a second. My skirt."

When he released her, she merely bent down, picked up her skirt by the hem and slipped it over her head. Sonia's petticoat suggested the *rhim,* but the *rhim*'s throat lacks the necklaces that adorned hers. She froze into immobility and, at once proud and frightened, looked him in the eye.

Her undergarments of the finest tissue and smooth as silk enveloped her body in tender bands.

"Do you want me to take off my stockings and my corset, or . . . do they excite you?"

He nodded. The phonograph played soft music. The woman joined her hands over the spot of her thighs and her whole body swayed gently to the rhythm of the waters. Her opulent breasts undulated to the same rhythm, a sight that would have given vigor to the most decrepit of cripples.

"That music is wonderful," she said, on the brink of esctasy.

"It's Spanish," said Madoubo.

"Is it functional?" she asked with interest.

"I have the idea it was composed as an accompaniment for lovemaking . . . to the rhythm of the guitars."

"A splendid idea," Sonia agreed with passionate sincerity.

Crawling to within fifty feet of them, Sankolo saw the woman do a slow, suggestive half-turn, raising her arms over her head and clapping her hands to the cadence of the music.

"My goodness," he heard her cry in a tone of impatience, "what kind of man are you, anyway?"

One leap took Madoubo within hand's grasp and his hand denied itself nothing.

On his face Sankolo felt the moist caress of the Yame. His harried heart beat like a compass needle gone wild. Moans poured from the truck. They were kissing. Suddenly Sankolo wanted to run and throw himself on the woman. But a dazed pain glued him to the spot. He saw Madoubo sniff at Sonia's breasts, seize them in hungry nervous lips, explore them and caress them with the tip of his tongue, the tips of his fingers. She lay strangely immobile, her head held stiffly. Frowning a little and sunk in the same lethargy as before. She caressed him. Sankolo tried to stretch out a hesitant arm. His muscles refused to obey. Brusquely he moved to one side, so as to be able to follow the couple's embraces in the rear-view mirror. He pulled the string of his trousers and instantly they fell. He lay down on his dashiki and, his eyes popping with desire at the splendor of Sonia's flesh, seized his own breasts, his lips, flung himself on his own body, his eyes riveted on their copulation. A throaty laugh sent the blood to his head, sent a tremor through his flanks which in his agitation had become entangled in his cotton dashiki, and he tore it. Suddenly he let out a jeering laugh and, spitting in his right palm, seized his member and pointed it at the couple:

"I've never had that. I'll torture my belly, I want to go to the extremity of love. Tell me, my member, have you seen the two white pigeons in the dovecote? How about it? Go in, see how that wooded treasure over the frieze of those white legs is reflecting your look. Go ahead, devour with your strong greedy lips the taut arc of that blond scented copse, where you, my treasure, lie sleeping. Again!" he panted, leaping into the air. "Oh! again, I beg you, kiss her. Peck, lick, lightning that strikes my entrails and releases the aureole of my belly. Look, my boobies, oh, my little clit, don't you love them? Keep it up . . . there . . . yes, there, taste her flesh, her real flesh, make me vomit the delight of her orgasm. This is what you like, isn't it? You enjoy it, don't you?"

And he purred under his own caresses, writhing in all directions, rubbing his legs together—and all his flesh vibrated like the string of a harp adroitly plucked, tenderly caressed. Every fiber of him was piercing delight; he let his fingers leap and frolic over his member, that little goblin, erect and pugnacious, they welcomed the copious warm dew that made him gurgle and moan with pleasure in the magnificent tumult of his total joy. With his rasping tongue he licked his hand and rubbed his body with saliva, keeping his eyes fixed on the bloody lips of the vulva in the rear-view mirror. And he began to sob softly. . . .

He sensed a presence behind him. He turned around: Awa, his fiancée, was watching him.

Sankolo lowered his eyes and looked at her. Instantly he knew that this woman detested him. Concentrating all his strength on giving pain, he closed his ears to all irrelevant sounds, to the breathing of the couple enlaced in the truck, to the drop of saliva oozing from the corner of his mouth—and stared at his fiancée, intent on drinking in all her jealousy and hate.

The courtesan stood out against the billowing Yame, whence the storks arose in white streamers; he knew she was bewildered, desperate—that she needed him—that he was going to inflict pain.

She looked at him with horror, the first man whose death agony she had felt inside her. Her breath caught in her throat. In a gross, hideous gesture, he pressed his thumb on his member and shook it aggressively. Then, naked, he stood up.

There was a great freshness in his body, the sensation of something dancing in his nostrils, the taste of blood in his throat which inflated with dry air.

Sankolo never knew that he had laughed in spite of his asphyxia; but because he could feel his heart beating in his very eyelids, and because she was going to die, his consciousness returned for the fraction of a second, as though his brain had been a shattered mirror capturing a fugitive light. His resolution welled up in the form of an intolerable pain. As though he had to be delivered of that pain as a mother is delivered of her child, a sob escaped him. Then brusquely taking a step, he expelled his pain and followed his child into a desolate waste.

He struck Awa a light blow on the cheek. She raised her hands in defense. He struck her full on the mouth, looking away with one eye, at the couple disporting themselves in the truck. That gave him a terrible air of detachment, as though to destroy Awa he needed only half his will.

He went on striking her haphazardly, absently—less interested in punishing her than in making blood flow and inflicting pain. Awa's hands were of no use to her; she made no attempt to return the blows, she loved him, she was tortured by the horror and degradation of this physical struggle. A fist descended on her nose, and she crumpled. She didn't say a word, thinking in her desperation: "He'll stop, he loves me, he doesn't want to commit murder."

Sankolo waited until she had got up, then with a sardonic smile he stroked his penis. The woman bucked him in the stomach. He staggered—a black stump—in the mud and bird droppings of the shore. A moan fell silent as Sankolo fought to recapture the impetus of his rage. Not that he recognized that voice: it was no more the voice of his fiancée than of any other woman moaning in endless despair, in infinite suffering and reproach.

"No! . . . No!" she gasped.

He hit the back of her head, pressed muck into her mouth, and went on striking. She tried to cry out. Sankolo listened. It was only a muffled groan that gave him no satisfaction. She wept; pain was a bird of prey fluttering more and more frantically from vein to vein in the body that imprisoned it. Awa opened her mouth as though to let the bird escape, she opened it wide, but the talons scraped her entrails and came back again relentlessly, piercing, tearing.

"If I could only faint," she thought, "if I could only cry out." And her hand clutched at the rivulet of black water that flowed down to the Yame, purpling and thickening with blood.

The bird stopped flitting about in her brain; in resignation it nestled in one corner of its prison. Into this pain Sankolo's words dripped slowly. She felt each one of them leave the man's lips, and her body winced in terror as she waited for the sound that would pierce her like an assegai at the base of her skull. When Sankolo approached, the bird woke up; the walls of Awa's brain vibrated, and the light touch of her lover's breath burned her like dung in an open wound.

Sankolo seized Awa by the throat. His knife whirled, twice he planted it in her left breast, slitted her belly from top to bottom. Suddenly expelled, her pink viscera crackled. He didn't even know whether the woman had screamed. He licked the blade, put the knife away in his belt. Covered the corpse with a wall of mud.

A shape vanished in the tall grass: Kassoumi, on his way home from the banana tree, had seen it all. *Alif minpitjè!*

### 5

Denounced by Kassoumi, repudiated by the notables, imprisoned by Vandame, Sankolo was banished by Saif, who, shrewd ideologist that he was, raised (to avenge himself for the scandal created by the murder of Awa) the prices on the Negro art exchange, cooking up, to the sauce of tradition and its "human values," a stew of pure symbolic religious art which he sent to Vandame, who passed it on to his correspondents who (may the Lord bless their innocence) peddled it to the curiosity seekers, tourists, foreigners, sociologists, and anthropology-minded colonials who flocked to Nakem. Qualities of lax, sterile, anachronistic redundancies; henceforth Negro art was baptized "aesthetic" and hawked in the imaginary universe of "vitalizing exchanges."

"Ever so often," Saif improvised, "the tools used to carve a mask were blessed seventy-seven times by a priest, who, all the while flagellating himself, gave blessings until the third day of the seventh year after the tree to be felled was chosen amid incantations revealing the genesis of the world."

"The plant," Shrobenius went on, "germinates, bears fruit, dies, and is reborn when the seed germinates. The moon rises to fullness, pales, wanes, and vanishes, only to reappear. Such is the destiny of man, such is the destiny of Negro art: like the seed and the moon, its symbolic seed is devoured by the earth and is reborn sanctified—imbued with the power requisite to its fulfillment—in the sublime heights of the tragic drama of the cosmic play of the stars." Negro art found its patent of nobility in the folklore of mercantile intellectualism, *oye, oye, oye.* . . .

But the audience of the All-Powerful is infinite; to the vast satisfaction of all concerned, He inspired Shrobenius to make known—a notion stamped with the genius of lunacy—the civilization and past of Nakem: "But these people are disciplined and civilized to the marrow! On all sides wide, tranquil avenues where we breathe the grandeur, the human genius of a people . . . It was only when white imperialism infiltrated the country with its colonial violence and materialism that this highly civilized people fell abruptly into a state of savagery, that accusations of cannibalism, of primitivism, were raised, when on the contrary—witness the splendor of its art—the true face of Africa is the grandiose empires of the Middle Ages, a society marked by wisdom, beauty, prosperity, order, nonviolence, and humanism, and it is here that we must seek the true cradle of Egyptian civilization."

Thus drooling, Shrobenius derived a twofold benefit on his return home: on the one hand, he mystified the people of his own country who in their enthusiasm raised him to a lofty Sorbonnical chair, while on the other hand he exploited the sentimentality of the coons, only too pleased to hear from the mouth of a white man that Africa was "the womb of the world and the cradle of civilization."

In consequence the niggertrash donated masks and art treasures by the ton to the acolytes of "Shrobeniusology." O Lord, a tear for the childlike good nature of the niggertrash! Have pity, O Lord! . . . *Makari! makari!*

Secreting his own myth, Shrobenius molded his personality: brilliant but easygoing, waggish but pessimistic, attentive to his publicity—but scoffing at a society that had given him everything.

This salesman and manufacturer of ideology assumed the manner of a sphinx to impose his riddles, to justify his caprices and past turnabouts. And shrewd anthropologist that he was, he sold more than thirteen hundred pieces, deriving from the collection he had purchased from Saif and the carloads his disciples had obtained in Nakem free of charge, to the following purveyors of funds: the Musée de l'Homme in Paris, the museums of London, Basel, Munich, Hamburg, and New York. And on hundreds of other pieces he collected rental, reproduction, and exhibition fees. "We often hear," he perorated in the castle that Negro art had earned him, "of the universe of this, that, or the other Nakem ethnos. The universe of Nakem is a familiar setting, the inner landscape which the people bear constantly within them, in which they find their true selves, from which they derive new strength. Thus the Nakem artist has no universe. Or rather, his universe is a vast solitude; no: a series of solitudes. . . ."

If anyone pointed to the contradiction between this solitude and the cosmological religiosity of the symbols from which Fritz molded the Negro artist, the anthropologist replied that the other had "failed to grasp his intention," which, however, he hastened to transmogrify. . . .

An Africanist school harnessed to the vapors of magicoreligious, cosmological, and mythical symbolism had been born: with the result that for three years men flocked to Nakem—and what men!—middlemen, adventurers, apprentice bankers, politicians, salesmen, conspirators—supposedly "scientists," but in reality enslaved sentries mounting guard before the "Shrobeniusological" monument of Negro pseudosymbolism.

Already it had become more than difficult to procure old masks, for Shrobenius and the missionaries had had the good fortune to snap them all up. And so Saif—and the practice is still current—had slapdash copies buried by the hundredweight, or sunk into ponds, lakes, marshes, and mud holes, to be exhumed later on and sold at exorbitant prices to unsuspecting curio hunters. These three-year-old masks were said to be *charged with the weight of four centuries of civilization.* To the credulous customer, the seller pointed out the ravages of time, the malignant worms that had gnawed at these masterpieces imperiled since time immemorial, witness their prefabricated poor condition. *Alif lam! Amba, koubo oumo agoum.*

## 6

Two days ago—*wassalam!*—Sankolo was released from prison. He hadn't seen Saif for three years. On this first day of February of the year of grace 1913, he runs into the learned Moses ben Bez Tubawi, whom he greets with the innocence of a wild beast and the placidity of a tree. Now he knows: Saif has chosen the better part of valor: he has shut himself up in his palace, whose gates are closed to Sankolo.

Sankolo, Kratonga, and Wampoulo have renewed their acquaintance, established mutual confidence through those precious silent halts known to lovers of the bush.

For a week they take the same zigzagging path that skirts the Yame, cutting across the boulder-strewn hollow traversed here and there by a trickle of water. The sky trembles in the sulphurous fuming heat, and under it the three men, lashed by the sun, stroll chatting.

. . . And then, early one morning, Sankolo died. He was buried at nightfall.

In the country swarming with humanity, a hundred serfs died in the early morning and were buried at nightfall. *Alif minpitjè!*

Amid peace and order serfs, domestics, laborers—many a robust son of the common people—died. A tear on their tombs.

Six months later, on the eve of the fourteenth of July, a parody of a man, emaciated, filthy, moving in short hops, hiccuping with his whole body when he spoke, appeared before Vandame.

He claimed that his name was Sankolo and that he had escaped. Vandame questioned his wife out of the corner of his eye and motioned the stranger not to move. Under the seal of secrecy, he sent for Kouyati, a sentry, who recognized Sankolo in the wreck. So he wasn't dead! Hadn't they buried him?

"Oh yes. Oh yes."

"Then what is this nonsense?"

Sankolo writhed, but rhythmically, obviously possessed. A few seconds later he was rolling on the ground, cursing, thrashing his legs; hoarse, never-ending, abysmal cries poured from his throat. He asked for something to drink. They gave him a glass of water, which he drained.

Then as though by enchantment, he sank into a state of wellbeing, his reason returned, though he still seemed under a spell. And he explained to Vandame—through Karim Ba, the interpreter—that he had been buried alive, then removed from his grave, drugged, and sent to the East to work for a Flencessi, Jean-Luc Dalbard, who dosed him with women and drugs, passed him off as dead, and finally sent him to the South, to Tal Idriss, a friend of Saif, to whom in exchange Tal was to send *his* living corpses. All those people who had died in the last six months, Sankolo revealed, were zombies like himself: living corpses enslaved, used as unpaid labor by Blacks and Whites, and ultimately shipped to Arabia as slaves at times when the normal supply was low:

"I have an incurable disease. Nothing can save me. Every time I drink, I feel the sweetness of lucid peace and the delicious torture of drugs. Dread quivers in my body like a cigarette in the mouth of a man condemned to death. My face twitches. I start howling again. People listen in silence; each one of them seems lost in himself. Our races are being brought together by music and drugs. A few Blacks. A few Whites; in the background shadows. Mulattoes. Gamblers, a rooster, a sorcerer. He distributes puffs of incense.

"My face twitches, contracts, with a crackling of music, now soft, now violent. In this music we recognize one another. Jean-Luc Dalbard and his friends Huot-Marchand, Eugène Blanchard, and Jean Martinon appropriate our sensibility. They are afraid. In this circle where sex is sin and paradise, they seem to be afraid of finding themselves inferior. And when their fear becomes intolerable, they frolic. They grasp black women by the breasts. With an expression at once romantic and cynical. Apparently they are trying to return to an elementary mode of life in which everything is reduced to the enjoyment of a few essential pleasures.

"My face stretches. I can't see anything. I scream. I drop. All listen to me in silence. I fall into a trance. I crawl over to the rooster and eat it alive, breaking its neck with a snap of my teeth. I say inaudible words. At certain moments my whole body is seamed with wrinkles. A strange, sweet sensation invades me: I wish I could escape from the sounds inside me, I feel strangely detached from them. Escape into nothingness. But how? I haven't the strength; I love the lethargy that envelops me little by little. The void creeps into me. My body loses all weight. The earth turns and with it the room, the people, their faces; their images seep into me as rain seeps into the freshly plowed earth. Old habits seize me by the member. A woman steps forward, black, beautiful, naked, her breasts are two enormous overturned flowers, whose cut stems exude a milky sap. Her belly, soft and voluptuous, dances toward me. She lies down on smoking coals and I possess her. Insensible to the pain, she nibbles me, her fluttering lashes sprinkle me with glances. She pants. Claws me and screams her orgasm. Writhes on the ground while, with me still erect inside her, we munch viper bones and broken bottles. The sound of our chewing mingles with the clapping and stamping of the onlookers. She vanishes. Trance. I rise, child born of the thrill of her firm flesh, take a few steps and stop, surprised to feel the weight of my body on the hard ground. Crush without seeing whether the face is sneering or loving. Kill without bothering to ask whether it's spleen or truth. Saif, I'll snatch your idol away from you.

"Weariness. My inattentive gaze curls up voluptuously over the void, as though in defiance. An inner voice dictates to me. The music oozes drop by drop from the drumskin. It rolls in the silence. Unconsciously my limbs mime the music, follow its inner dictation, known to all. Go into the room next door. Melt into her and run away with her. Go beyond the known, discover the caress of the sea fern. With my soul that will dream of flaming silence, of a green sun setting on a purple sea with golden, narcotic shores. Go away to be with the others, whose tormented faces twitch and contract like mine, and then vanish into the room next door. See nothing. Never again. Forget. Or choose. But why?

"Slowly my fingers play over my face; caress it like a woman's body. A light has entered the shadows of my face. That's the wood fire. The end. I enter the room. Next door. Graveyard of the hours of folly. . . .

"Suddenly a door slams loudly; I turn around. A beam of light blinds my eyes. Someone is bending over me, a voice buzzes in my head, I remember fears conversing in distant corridors. The light goes out with a click. I breathe darkness through my mouth and nostrils, a darkness peopled with cries.

"Far from the frail straw huts and the great smoky fires, my life begins again; but I have consumed my strength enduring misery. Suddenly I am born out of despair, I throw myself on the ground, tear my hair, then standing I slowly strew the beads of a rosary on the earth and they give me the strength to begin again. . . . To begin again for three successive days. My life resumes. My battle is silent. It bites the silence. Night. Silence. And then night.

". . . At last the third night is coming. The last. I wait. I listen. Light and shade in the room. I don't move. The man is approaching. I know. I don't resist. They are burning wood. They take a bull carved from wood. Now there are seven in the room. The sorcerer holds the bull in his hands. The bull is God. The man approaches, gouges stripes on my wrists, my forearms, with the sharp horn. There is no longer much blood on my skin. The blood oozes. A vein is pierced. The blood spouts, spouts. . . . It drips down onto the purifying coals, crackles, bursts like a sob in a prayer. There is a roaring in my head, an exasperating ringing in my ears, it shatters my eardrums. The pain concentrates in a single point, in the back of my head. They are moving me, dragging me, I can sense it. My nostrils are drunk with the smell of my burned blood. My hands are avid for air, a flame that will dry my blood. I am no longer in pain. A flow of murmurs in which the whole world dances, hovers, trembles, suddenly bursts into a blaze, and collapses. . . . I sink into a sticky torpor.

"I have just won—at that moment for the first time—the right to live. Saif, I will snatch away your idol!

"I undress. I sprinkle myself with water gathered in my two hands. Trembling. Hollow. Hungry. I proceed slowly, almost calmly. At a certain stage of fatigue, to be despondent, dirty or clean, is all one. I wash myself. Ritual. A man is watching me. I know it without even thinking. I'll stay here an hour more, then I'll leave. That will be the end. Witnesses will swear. Been paid for it. They will swear that they saw me die, that they were deeply grieved when the hands of death crushed my soul after the ritual, orgiastic ceremony they had honored me with. And for the second time I shall be dead. Cheap labor is needed. Sold without having been bought, I shall work without pay. Somewhere else. For Saif's friend Tal Idriss, who will send *his* corpse here to work. They've sold me good and proper. An exchange. That's all. An exchange of favors that will drive us all mad, with this obsessive music in our rest periods, this frenzy to work in order to possess those sixty sensual women, this drug that is eating away our last fibers. . . . The simple souls who countenance and justify the perfidy of man put it down to fetishism.

Voodoo. Or some other aberration. Mad. Dead. I shall be absent from the world. I've been sold good and proper.

"The water is warm. With a motion of the hand I ask for soap. I crumble it. It's local soap, black, friable, and greasy, made of local materials. I soap myself. The water in the tin bucket reflects my image. Emaciated. Unshaven. Less human than ever. With swollen lips.

"I muddle the image. I lift the bucket. Higher. Over my head. The water pours down. The soap, the filth, the oily smell leave me. The water drips. My skin is alive, alive again. I wipe my limbs with my curved fingers. I wait. The water dries. The sun drinks the last little drops on my body. Now I'm clean. I slip into the white cotton blouse they give me. I crack the joints of my toes. I walk. With nervous feet. Bare. Chapped. Flat on the ground.

"I leave the clay mound where I washed. I go down to the man. Impassive. He gives me an ax. A game bag. With crushed millet in it. Ropes. A piece of fine cloth. White. Square; a handkerchief. It will serve to strain the water I drink on the way. The cloth will keep me from drinking too much dirt. I have no machete. But a pocket knife.

"The man goes away. He gives an order. They bring me food. I want to sit down on the ground but they tell me I have to go off to one side. A hundred yards away. More to the south. I should eat and leave the calabashes. A domestic will come for them. Then, they explain, I must be on my way. Southward, always southward. Along the river. In three nights I shall arrive. They're expecting me. . . .

"I think the word: sold. And my thoughts move toward an explanation that I am unwilling to accept. Sold . . . And what if I escape! I'm alone.

"A hundred yards away I sit down. I'm weak with hunger. I eat. Slowly. I don't want to give up for lack of strength. I don't want to die. No . . . I swallow a mouthful. And catch myself doubting what has happened to me. Drugged. Sequestered. Me

. . . there's no law. There's money, and people want it at any price. Saif, aaah! When my nostrils burrow into my soul, when your crimes rise up naked, my sarcastic fury rages and jeers at you.

"I chew. I think: *It's drugged*. The spice whets my appetite. My thirst. I drink. I eat, kneading the rice between my numb, trembling fingers. My fingers recapture old habits. My stomach relaxes. A monkey looks at me. He yaps. I can't listen to him. I'm hungry. It makes me drunk to recover my strength, to feel myself reborn from hunger. My nimble fingers feed me. I take a long swig of palm wine. A pause. I drink again. Then the gourd is empty. I rinse my gums with my forefinger and a mouthful of water. Another mouthful: my meal is over. I get up. The domestic comes and takes the empty dishes.

"Southward. I hold the ax. I start off. Along the river . . .

"Always this same landscape that I seem to recognize with its floating tree trunks, its animal cries, its colors, its light which bewilders and astonishes the eyes. The hardships of the march, this depressing forest with its dancing vapors of heat and humidity. Flowing water turns out to be a chant in the ears of a sleepwalker. For long hours my arms have struck ax blows at the lianas. I trudge on. Blindly southward. As though fascinated, hypnotized.

"My food was drugged with *dabali*. But what does it matter? I'm alive. I'm walking. That's all. I respond to an inner mechanism, an imperious command. Southward. Southward. They're expecting me. I'm thirsty. The earth is spinning. My tongue feels like a balloon. My thirst is unbearable. I'll drink in a little while. But not enough to make me sluggish. There's plenty of water. The river for miles and miles. I'll drink when I want to. I've got to keep going. The wild fruit reminds me of greenery, the greenery speaks of water, the water makes my thirst thirstier. I'll drink in a little while. I've got to keep going. As much as water, what my body wants is my drugged millet, my private sedative. Southward. I've got to obey. In a little while, when I've got through those lianas I'll have a right to drink. There. Here I am. Just a little farther. There. At last I can drink. I take out my handkerchief. I set it to my lips. I suck in the water, I savor it in little sips. I chew my millet, I drink. . . . It's good, it's cool and soft as the caress of a flower. . . .

"I get up. Southward. Southward. My body is floating. My legs are pedaling. My arms are thrashing. But it's not me. I feel good. An angel is carrying me. I feel good. The trees are green, the water is quicksilver, I'm a jeweler. I make jewels with sunbeams. I give them to the birds, which have white feathers and green eyes sprinkled with stars, and the birds follow me; they make music for the pleasure of my senses. At my feet, surrounded by a cortege of kettledrums and lovesick flutes, half-dressed women with silk shawls that hide their thighs. There are brunettes, three—swathed in white wool; and blondes, two—dressing themselves with their golden hands; a redhead—bedecking herself with flowers, green leaves, and grapes. And black women in a circle, with neither dresses nor jewels nor sandals. And cat-eyed Asiatic women, whose hair—black of their black—and mouths—pink of their pink—hover around me, as light and round as feathers. . . . Their provocative smile clutches my member, which stiffens and points up at one of them, it swings my feet in the void—and I possess the whole lot of them. My arms come and go, speak to the wind, I fly and glide over a carpet of red-brown grass as soft as down caressed by the breeze. Stars and planets pour from my fingers. A sudden gust of wind lifts me up high in the air: I see cities, whole peoples from all four corners of the earth, prodigiously elongated, with the legs of storks and human faces sculptured by myself. Suddenly I see the white man who sold me and had me drugged, and I speak to my enslaved brothers. They're very little, very black, with indistinguishable features. I speak to them, I tell them I'm going to work for nothing, officially dead, a dog drugged by the scum of the earth—and I see that they're looking in Saif's direction and weeping. Suddenly I'm holding a scepter. I stop the secret war over money. Saif is destroyed under the lava. Money is dead. I stop everything. I raise my scepter: lions step forward shaking their manes, in which all the women I've possessed, all the men I've bullied, are strutting about. The niggers rise again. The Jews rise again. In rising, all the oppressed save the essence of themselves. The wind looks at them, the silence listens to them. The sky is indigo-black and I stand out against an azure background fallen from the clouds. I give orders, my speech has the power of the Word. I am lowered to the ground. I move. I walk. I smile without moving my lips. The river follows me. The water follows me. The sun dances to my steps. My steps are light, they crisscross in the landscape, forming designs beneath my enormous shadow, arches, holy places, enigmas which I alone decipher in the presence of the amazed forest. The trees stop talking, their branches part to let me pass. My ax is merciless, it strikes all those who are jealous. A lion pants, he has come a long way: he stands before me. He roars, sticks out his tongue, walks away backwards and vanishes over the horizon. He perches on a treetop, turns into a superb pink panther with fiery glowing jaws, licked by flames:

"It is the sun that is setting.

"My head.
"My head.
"My God, the pain. I'm tired. What is there in the South? My tongue is so heavy. It's an enormous block of ice. Painfully I savor my icy tongue and my limbs aroused by its coldness. My body is black. My body is a vault filled with an avalanche of cold shivers clinging to tatters of sound. Nature speaks; she's hot. I am king, I live the life of the privileged. The crickets cry out with the heat, I am frozen with intense pleasure. I'm in pain. I don't want to be the victim of my obsessions. I am a sick field. My head rolls after the lianas in the sperm-wet ground. My eyes go on clearing the forest. In the landscape a few trees refuse to stand: they lie down in ditches, drift, slide, stop for a moment at the wall of the horizon as a moth stops at a lamp.

"My eyes aim at the infinite. The sun goes to sleep. It is still far away. It's afraid of falling. It's a timorous pink panther, trembling behind the dunes and the blue valleys. My headache is a barnyard. Ferocious. With its cries, its familiar sights, its sudden flapping of wings, its squawking. At the edge of the barnyard begins a desert of greenery that rasps my mucous membranes. Suddenly everything is extraordinary and monotonous.

"I ask the earth to stop moving, to let me rest without anguish, my body no longer a clenched fist in the gaping wound of the sunset. At every instant I collapse into it, at every step, every movement, with sun in my head, with waves in my body, crashing one after another. At the bottom of this downfall I go forward in silence, with weary legs and trembling arms. The path turns into an immense vagina. My death, nothingness; my body blots out the light so thoroughly that I exist in a state of reprieve, thanks only to sensations that never express me and always save me. The forest resembles abandoned limbs. A rubber tree tugs at its roots, eager to go away. I am a sniffing animal. I smell wine and the presence of a palm tree. I make an incision, drink the palm wine, chew my drugged millet that makes me thirsty. I drink, again the drug takes effect. And I plod through the darkness, cutting, slashing, my eyes dilated. I see nothing. Neither road nor path. Night. I don't like these trails; they are all the same, without character; with slung rifles they walk in a special way, legs straight, body stiff as a board, head over there, a makeshift path. The silence sleeps, dreaming of the sky where the clouds envy the moon. Here's the bank of the Yame River, with its black swell, its dampness. The river. Southward. Southward. I've got to. They're expecting me. Why sleep? Maybe I've arrived. I run to catch myself, I follow myself at a gallop. I stop, body erect, arms stretched forward. I'm like a lemon without juice. I can't see myself any more. Neither my hands nor my limbs. Sleep. I'm afraid of the snakes. Sleep. Dream. Sleep. I'm afraid of the red ants. I don't want to be eaten. I wish I could turn into an animal and survive this menacing forest, its mosquitoes, its flies, those black things that crawl out of its belly in the darkness. Fire. I want fire. With fire I'll fear nothing. The snakes will go away. The rabbits will go away. The monkeys will chatter. The animals will think I'm armed. I'll be saved. I'll wait till daylight. Only then will I sleep.

"The night crushes me so with its procession of indefinable sensations that I *become* the wind, the silence of nature, its fears, its darkness, its expectation. I try to become nature more entirely, to melt into it, to become one with it and to fear its intolerable darkness no longer. My fire snaps and crackles. The sparks cast a shifting yellowness about me. Insects hum a tune around the fire. Blinking phosphorescent eyes. Fireflies perhaps. Or cats' eyes. The branches speak, hoot, hide behind my back. I'm afraid. I hold my ax in my hand. I turn. I pace on springy legs. Spongy legs, my body sinks into them, I struggle to tear myself away from them. Under my heels the ground becomes hard, hot, crumbly. My breathing is raucous. My eyes are two round onions. Tears dance in them but never roll down my cheeks. Unbearable but necessary insomnia. I want to live.

"The landscape dances. My eyelashes paint it, cut it up into needles, into granite, into spurs eroded by the wind, into masses of foliage whence a vapor rises skyward. Swarms of twinkling sparks collapse into a hole of aching clouds, jostled and gesticulating, then rigid, stiff with fatigue.

"That's a bad moon. Lusterless. Treacherous. I have a foreboding of something. A living presence, but it's hiding. A crackling of branches. No. Nothing. The wind. Five minutes. A sound. In the darkness a shape, smooth, massive, lurking—three paces away. I yell, lash it with my ropes, jump. The shape rolls to one side. Dodges, cursing. I throw myself on it, groping for my ax. A violent twist throws me off balance and for half an instant a face appears before me: wide, flat, glistening. With wild eyes under a visor of bushy hair, a mouth torn by an uneven row of teeth. Pointed. Yellow and doglike.

"The man, a Nakemian, has the same scars as I, regular, sunk deep into his forehead. We're of the same tribe. I speak to him.

He speaks to me. He tells me my name: Sankolo. Then his: Tandou. Silence.

"He sits down by the fire. He too has an ax, ropes, a game bag, just like me. But he's going north. He chews his millet drugged with *dabali*. He takes quantities of it. He asks me for a handful of my millet. To compare, he says. I object, I say I'm out of it. The man bargains. I give him a little millet for a little information. About my future boss. About the working conditions. About life in the South, where he's come from. 'You'll see,' he says. 'They won't ask you any questions. Work, eat, work: don't say anything. Don't talk back. Good morning, good night, that's all. You'll have your women and your drugs.'

"The man laughs. He cries. A long time, in silence. As if he were trying with his tears to recover from his exhaustion, from the mental anesthesia that made him resemble an animal. He needed to resume contact with the core of himself. Deep in thought, he talks. He explains; he listens to himself speak.

" 'We'll never get through.'

" 'What?'

" 'The wall.'

" 'What wall?'

" 'That wall . . . there . . . there,' he raves. 'Don't you see, a nigger is nothing; a nigger woman is good enough to fuck. We're helpless; we haven't got the law on our side. There's Saif, it's a country without many witnesses: so they sell us. Oh, horrible,' he sobs. Then suddenly with gentle resignation: 'But you'll see, you'll forget everything with *dabali*. Yes . . . you too, you'll forget.'

" 'I'll be alone. A man thinks when he's alone. I'll never be able to forget . . . never!'

" 'You're dead. *Dead,* do you understand?! You've got no proof, no papers, nothing!'

" 'And the authorities?'

" 'What authorities?'

" 'The census. The police.'

" 'What about them?'

" 'There's still hope.'

" 'You're *dead,* can't you see that? You'll work in the South for two years. Two years and three months. When the police and the census takers come, they'll send you to the East. You'll be so completely drugged you won't be able to answer, you'll howl like an animal, your dilated eyes will want women, and everybody will run away from you. You'll have just two words in your head: *dabali*-work, work-*dabali*. Once in a while a whore will make love to you. And then . . . you know the end: madness. Bah! . . . We only die once. Give me some millet.'

"I give him some. Kill myself? What for? . . . Maybe it's just a nigger's life. Slave. Sold. Bought, sold again, trained. Thrown to the winds. . . . They need cheap labor.

"The man gets up. We put out the fire. In silence. Day is breaking. We skirt the river, our enlarged, tired shadows walk beside us in its dirty mirror. The man turns off to the North; it's a little as if I myself had died. I start southward, without looking back."

For reasons of security Vandame kept Sankolo in his house, settling him in a room adjoining his study, where he himself kept watch. On leaving Vandame, Karim Ba ate a hasty dinner, then went to Tillabéri-Bentia to inform Saif.

Eleven P.M. Saif sent for Kratonga and Wampoulo. When they had come: "Muss him up a bit."

Karim Ba was terrified. "But we made a deal," he protested.

"Suppose it was a trap?" Saif insinuated in a toneless voice.

Karim began to moan, his plaint trembled in the lull of the wind; the tears glistened in his eyes. Croaking with terror, he prepared to evade the first blow, thinking that Kratonga would move slowly.

The attack took Karim by surprise. Kratonga struck with astounding speed and precision. The interpreter crumpled, only to be lifted up by a kick. And while Kratonga held Karim still, Wampoulo crouched, gauged the distance, and shot out his right heel. The interpreter bellowed, his face contorted with pain, he clutched his belly in both hands. The two men beat him like a mule, the blood spurted from his nose, his mouth, his ears. Saif set his foot on Karim's forehead and the agents stepped aside. Saif made as if to trample the man with all his weight, then, having scared him out of his wits, moved slowly back.

"In any case," said Saif, "you had no choice. Vandame couldn't have found out anything without his dear interpreter, could he? Of course, Karim, you didn't have to come. But your dropping in like this shows what good care you take of your family. Well, right now I want you to enjoy yourself. I want to see you smile. And hear you laugh. Go on!"

Karim started laughing softly, nervously, hesitantly, as though it were something very difficult that he was doing for the first time. But encouraged by Saif's look of approbation, his laughter took on a note of hilarity—swelled to a wheezing bleat. Saif smiled and filed his nails. Only Wampoulo and Kratonga remained grave. Finally Karim stopped to catch his breath. Still huddled on his knees, he gasped avidly for air. Suddenly Saif's face turned cold and impassive.

The truth burst into the room just as Saif had planned. Drooping pitifully, immobilized by Kratonga's dagger, Karim Ba looked down as though afraid to face the fascinating glitter of the steel.

"Go ahead," Saif ordered. "Repeat what Sankolo said."

"I beg you," Karim Ba moaned. "I implore you . . ."

Kratonga's dagger flashed through the air, grazing the clot of bloody spittle in the corner of the interpreter's mouth.

"It's the truth," Karim bellowed hysterically. "It's the truth. Vandame is guarding him in his study. You've got to believe me! It's not a trap. . . ."

His sentence ended in a sob and he vomited up his dinner.

"Now tell us how to go about it."

Slowly the interpreter raised his head. He looked up at the self-satisfied Saif, he saw Kratonga put his dagger away, and as though waking from a nightmare he realized to his consternation that he had signed the governor's death sentence.

"Here!" said Saif, throwing him two packets of bank notes.

———

Wampoulo had put the sentry's dog to sleep with drugged meat. The sentry himself was snoring at his post five hundred yards from the governor's residence.

Kratonga threw a handful of gravel at Vandame's window. A clicking of pebbles. Then nothing.

Wampoulo joined him on the run. Both huddled behind the door and waited. Still nothing. Vandame was too smart. Then Kratonga stood up, walked away backwards, and hid behind a tree. From there he directed his flashlight at the window of the room where Sankolo was sleeping. A sound of chairs being moved: frightened, Sankolo opened the door to take refuge with Vandame. Wampoulo caught him and gagged him. Vandame came out. Automatic in hand. No one. He made the circuit of the house. Something hit him on the head: he lost consciousness.

When he came to, he was tied to a jogging horse. Jolting over a stony path not far from the Yame, they were skirting a waterfall that could not be seen from the road. Kratonga ordered Wampoulo to help Vandame down. He himself tied the horses to a tree, deposited the governor's automatic on a rock, and sat down.

The water fell in dense ivory folds, enveloping them in its roar, and suddenly they were thousands of years from civilization. Bats circled in the half-light, and the eeriness of the sound was enhanced by the moon which spread milky sheets over the Yame.

Vandame rubbed the back of his head and grimaced. He had on Chinese slippers with thick felt soles, black satin pajama pants, and an embroidered Chinese tunic with a white plastron. He stood very straight, holding his knees close together; his body maintained a military posture. Over his long chin his teeth glistened between his lips. His eyes were wide open, and the slate color of his pupils seemed to invade his irises. Eyes of madness. He appeared to be quite unconscious, yet was anything but unconscious.

In a voice betraying his nervousness he exploded:

"I'd never have thought Saif so unworthy of France."

Kratonga with a forced smile: "His Royal Magnificence reigns here below as the Lord All-Powerful. His edicts are inscribed in heaven. Woe to anyone who disobeys them: one fine morning he wakes up recalled to the Most-High."

Vandame was surprised to find that Saif's agents spoke French very well. Saif himself, he was soon to learn, expressed himself excellently in that language. But he declined to let it be known and insisted (so playing the game of the colonials unbeknownst to them) on using Karim Ba.

And Wampoulo abruptly: "I thought you Whites were clever. Excuse my mistake."

"I don't understand," the governor stammered.

"All right, Vandame," Wampoulo shot back. "Tell us what you don't understand." Slowly Wampoulo approached the governor. His tongue protruded a little from his teeth. Vandame made a visible effort to pull himself together. He smiled:

"I presume that you work for money, that you wouldn't want to share the fate of your associate. . . ."

"What associate?"

"Sankolo."

"You're investigating the case of Sankolo?"

"Oh, you know how it is. . . ."

"No, Vandame, I don't know how it is. Not in the least."

The governor shot a piercing glance at the two men:

"You're completely out of your minds," he said slowly, measuring his words. "You're angry because we've colonized you, because Saif and the rest of you are something like errand boys in the job we're doing in Nakem. That's why you play these tricks on us, and what dirty tricks." (Kratonga seemed impressed.) "You fellows started out as sons of the slaves, the captives my country is trying to liberate, to civilize—and here you are siding with the scum. . . . You want his insolence to go on forever, you're afraid of falling into disgrace!"

"It's all the fault of Lady Luck," said Wampoulo in what he thought was a tone of detachment. "The witch is seldom on our side. In our trade we're always trying to catch up with her, and we thumb our noses at her."

"You hang around with Saif because you like it," said Vandame feebly. "The life appeals to you, you just won't admit it."

"That's a crummy way to talk, pal. What's the matter with you? Moralizing when there's a chance to have a little fun?"

"Fun?"

"We're your new friends, pal. Treat your friends right, Vandame."

"Very well," said Vandame with an air of taking his misadventure philosophically. "We'll call it a friendly chat if you like."

For some moments he had been moving imperceptibly closer to the automatic. Kratonga had noticed, and so had Wampoulo no doubt. Suddenly Vandame pivoted, plunged headfirst at the rock, and seized the weapon. He aimed it at the two men and, in the awful daring of a moment's surrender, pulled the trigger, pulled it again, three times in succession. Then blood shook his heart; his hands slowed down and stopped. For a moment he lay on the rock as though exhausted. They could hear him panting. Then slowly he stood up in grim despair and turned to the two men with a pathetic smile.

"That was extremely rude of you, governor," said Kratonga, picking up the pistol and slipping in the magazine, after displaying it to the horrified Vandame.

From far off in the bush the muffled plaint of a hyena was heard. There was no end, only addition: Vandame was sweating profusely. He had made the first move; and now the silence around them hearkened to the footfalls of the unknown.

Kratonga went over to one of the horses and from the saddlebag removed a large bamboo cylinder and a waterskin. The governor turned around and, dying in his own death, whispered: "You're taking a terrible risk."

Kratonga flung the cylinder into the air: it spun whistling through the moonlight, described a semicircle, and struck the rock with a sound of splintering wood. Some sheets of paper fell out: the report that Vandame had just drawn up about Saif.

"I can give you a written statement. Sankolo's escape, my wife's testimony. We didn't see a thing, we don't know a thing." (Vandame was green, his lips kept moving.) "I thought I was doing my duty. I'll sign anything you please."

But Kratonga took the waterskin, opened it, took a gulp, then offered the rest to Wampoulo, who barely tasted it.

"Give it to Vandame."

"I'm not thirsty," the governor protested faintly.

"Who cares? You've got work to do."

"Rot!" cried Kratonga. "A strapping big chap like you isn't afraid of a drop. Well . . ."

Docile and obedient as a horse, Vandame looked from one to the other and finally complied. Raising the waterskin, closing his eyes as though the better to endure his torment. His flabby throat contracted at each gulp. The waterskin shrank. He almost made it. But his stomach rebelled. He staggered and fell to his knees. The waterskin slipped from his hands, the milk spilled. Vandame vomited on the hungry sand, then he slowly raised himself on his elbow. His face was a yellowish gray.

"You're in bad shape," said Kratonga. "You need something to set you up. A little drink, just a drop."

"I don't think I . . ."

"You're asking for trouble, Vandame. Go on, drink."

Kratonga came close to him. Vandame raised the waterskin, licked his lips, and opened his mouth. A viscous black ribbon slipped slowly from the skin and fell to the ground. Vandame was still trying, slowly, painfully, to coax a drop of milk when he suddenly heard a hissing and felt something cold touch his left calf. He looked down and froze with terror: an asp. His face went blue. The snake had coiled around his foot. He was reeling with fright when Kratonga whistled: "Dafa . . ."

The snake uncoiled and settled down three feet from the stunned, bewildered governor. "Lick her head," Wampoulo ordered. While he was hesitating, Kratonga kicked him in the behind. He tumbled so fast that when he picked himself up he was still teetering, with the snake at his heels, to recover his balance. Kratonga whistled and with a rustling of its scales the snake stopped still.

"Go on, lick it!"

The governor approached, recoiled in horror, but then, fearing the worst, began to lick the horned triangular head, while with her forked tongue Dafa, daughter of Tama, marked his face with sticky flashes.

"Do that every day and you'll live longer," said Kratonga. "Will you do it every day?"

"Yes, sir," said Vandame.

All resistance had gone out of him. He had accepted the humiliation; there wasn't much left of him, only a blind desire to see the light. The terror Saif's agents had succeeded in arousing in him had mounted steadily since he had pulled the trigger of his empty automatic.

"I can give you a statement," Vandame repeated.

These words were a kind of talisman; he chanted them like a prayer, without great hope.

"I can give you the whole thing in writing."

Suddenly Kratonga seized Dafa and threw her at Vandame. The asp thudded against his chest, fell to the ground and enlaced his legs.

"Undo the knot, Vandame. I love you, Vandame. You're the righteous man of colonialism. Move away from our excellent Wampoulo. A little more. That's it, friend. You're okay, pal. We're going to play William Tell. It's one A.M. *Allons enfants de la patrie.* It's the fourteenth of July, Governor. Pick up your report about His Royal Magnificence. Get a move on. That's the stuff. Roll it into a ball, Vandame. Put it on your head, Major."

Vandame's eyes seemed to pop out of his head.

"You can't . . ."

"Don't get excited. I'm a dead shot, pal. Go on. On your head. I love you, Vandame. Humanist, governor, friend of black freedom, civilizer of Nakem, family man, and republican!"

Vandame stood there with his eyes closed, his arms dangling.

His body was going out from under him. Hugging his knees: Dafa.

Kratonga ground his teeth. The barrel of the automatic described diminishing circles. Kratonga held it at arm's length and took meticulous aim.

The automatic gave a dry cough, muffled by the roaring of the waterfall. Vandame jerked convulsively and the report burst into flames. Wampoulo extinguished the blaze and replaced the report on the governor's head. Again Kratonga took aim. "Oh, Governor," he gasped. "I had such an awful dream. I dreamed about me. I thought some Whites were chasing me, and I couldn't run, and my neck was—oh, it was all covered with blood. Oh-h, I can't go on."

Vandame was seized with a panic terror, unreasoning, instinctive.

"Not a soul need know what's happened to us," Kratonga wailed. And his dry, passionate talk commanded attention.

For some time Vandame had not heard Wampoulo moving and had begun to wonder what he was doing.

When he sensed danger, he groped at shapes and ran because he could not stop for death. Suddenly Wampoulo clasped his shoulders and shook them so frantically that Vandame's neck swung and broke.

Quicker than speech, his arms waltzed above him, then rowed him softlier home, to the Artful Creator.

Blood spurted from the nape of his neck like reluctant rubies grasped by a beetle. His eyeballs like frightened beads, Vandame drank a dewdrop from a blade of grass. He was a righteous man.

Along with what remained of Vandame's report, Kratonga and Wampoulo, still in accordance with Saif's instructions, brought the governor's body back to his study, where they set it carefully in place.

When Sankolo, escorted by Kratonga and Wampoulo, found himself in Saif's presence, he knew he was to be sacrificed.

Making it clear to him that a refusal or the slightest false move would mean the death of Bineta, the natural child borne to him by Awa, his fiancée, they sent him back to the governor's residence.

Kouyati the sentry pretended not to see him: Kratonga and Wampoulo had bribed Kouyati and threatened to kill his family if he betrayed them.

It all went off as planned. Sankolo played the thief, come to steal the governor's money and Madame Vandame's finery; he paced her bedroom, marveling in a loud voice at her clothes and jewels, until she awoke with a start and cried out for help. At this he lost his head and fled, dropping the automatic. Just as Madame Vandame was making a rush for it, he doubled back into the room. A struggle for the weapon, cries; the gun went off. Madame Vandame collapsed. Automatic in hand, Sankolo took to his heels, wreaking havoc in Vandame's study on the way, so explaining the murder. In escaping he broke the window: Kouyati opened fire and riddled Sankolo's head with bullets. Vandame's automatic on the floor pointed unmistakably to Sankolo as the murderer.

Captain Mossé, his wife, their son Jean, Lieutenant Huygue, his wife, and most of the soldiers woke up and rushed in, bewildered, from all sides.

And Kouyati made it clear that he hadn't neglected his duty, that he hadn't been asleep, that he had fired on the unknown marauder whom the governor himself, touched by his misery, had taken in for one night. . . . Forgive us, O Lord. *Atchou hackè!*

Vandame and his wife lay in state for three days. Eighty thousand people filed past them, paying a last homage to these righteous people who, by virtue of their very purity, had taken no part in the politics of Nakem but had acquired a stainless reputation among the freed men and the administration.

Their silver-trimmed coffins were superb: the finely wrought angels at either end glowed in the golden light of the candles. Engraved on marble tablets, the inscription: *Honneur et Patrie.*

The burial in the Mt. Katsena cemetery was the most sumptuous that had ever been seen in Nakem. There were twenty-six carloads of flowers, half of them donated by Saif ben Isaac al-Heit. *Wakul rabbi zidni ilman!*

On his return to the palace Saif learned that the family of Lieutenant Huygue, whose daughter was confined at the Hôpital Saint-Anne in Paris, were leaving Nakem for good, bearing the hatred of Africa in their hearts.

Saif said: "Our Father who art in Heaven," and the birds chirped in response.

7

The Whites camped in the midst of their *tirailleurs,* in the midst of false lamentations. The Flencessi officers obtained obedience by disciplinary measures, blows, and shouting. In the disorder that ushered in the year 1914 numerous *tirailleurs* deserted, were reported missing, or were shot down by firing squads; great quantities of provisions, property, and wealth were lost. And on top of all this confusion the Great War—dancing chaos of the world's anger—broke out.

Despairing of his authority, no weakling but disarmed, Mossé, Vandame's successor, held long conferences with Saif ben Isaac al-Heit, in the course of which he showed his utmost consideration and respect. Unhoped-for favors and privileges were granted His Royal Magnificence. He promised to win the niggertrash to the cause of the army.

When, accordingly, the popular enthusiasm reached its height —*ya atrash!*—Saif ben Isaac al-Heit, with Madoubo at his side and his sorcerers behind him, addressed the crowd, crying out that he had parted company with his own body, that he had been superseded by the divine commandments, whose breath alone now issued from his mouth; a celestial voice, he announced to the *tirailleurs*—playthings of the wisdom of the invisible Master of the Worlds—that if they died in battle they would live again in their former tribes, "their souls sevenfold more pure than the dawn at the time of the morning prayer."

Cries spread far and wide through the woods, songs and the somber tom-tom carried messages, hawks flew through the air with messages in their talons, and Saif, a mage whose words took flight like holy papal bulls to descend on the herd of seraphically ecstatic niggertrash, negotiated with the Whites and obtained their promise not to touch a single hair of the heads of the notables' sons, who were thus exempted from conscription.

To lure the *tirailleurs,* avid for the splendors of Holy Paradise, the notables set themselves up as the saviors of the martial soul: kissing their gaudy-loinclothed better halves good-by, adorning their arms with talismans and their necks with heavy amulets upon which they looked down with gilded smiles, black men flocked to the army. There were serious disturbances, rebellions fomented by lucid men, though of low extraction—the stake awaits them!—shrieking: "These *tirailleurs*—aren't they just like the early Christian martyrs, who bleated their faith in eternal resurrection and marched into the jaws of the lions?"

But Saif, Commander of the Faithful, made the illuminated people see how contemptible it was to think instead of believing, and sent hordes of blustering bloodthirsty soldiers to Mossé, raised an army of able-bodied men armed with knives, hoes, iron-tipped staves, slings, and an occasional gun. And whipped into a frenzy of fanaticism by the sorcerers, all ran to their death with joy in their hearts, brandishing bulls' tails in their left hands and confident of resurrection.

More than one disappeared, "sold to Mecca," so the chronicles relate, spirited out of the ecstatic mob in which (Heaven protect us!) men were seen appropriating parts of cannon, clutching them in their embrace and letting themselves be killed without relaxing their grip, in their haste to sit down right next to the Eternal Father whose land is gold dust—and His river a blessing; others were seen thrusting their arms into the mouths of cannon to pull out the shells. The officers gave up in despair and sent for Saif, who quieted the niggertrash, restored order and discipline, and forbade all looting or excesses "on pain of

being turned away from the gates of the cool Kingdom on high."
"May we all be reunited one day," he chanted, "in the shadow
of the throne of the most-gentle Lord, in the spheres of Eden.
That is the grace I ask of Him. *Amina yarabi!"*

It would have been a simple matter to preach holy counter-
revolution and drown the power of those "helmeted apes" in
blood. But the niggertrash had already been freed and the notables tolerably indemnified; as Saif pointed out, it would be
risky to fight the Whites in time of world conflict: any return to
a feudal society based on slavery, the source of the notables'
prosperity, would involve civil war.

And so Saif, benefiting from as many miracles as he performed, appointed grand officer of the Legion of Honor, honored
as the "savior of France in Nakem," obtained regal pensions
for himself and his faithful. And mustering all their spiritual
resources, the notables prayed loudly for the *tirailleurs* and
the resurrection of the saints, professing themselves the
"guardians of their souls and the souls of the wives they have
left at home."

"Don't be in a hurry to meet the Most-High," Saif said to
them, "or He will punish you: a man can die of an itch for
immortality. Therefore be good soldiers, fight and wait, for
Heaven will not come to you until God has granted you salvation and given you His blessing. My gentle lambs, let us praise
the Lord for the abundant favors and benefits He has heaped
upon us by making us His devoted worshipers, so preserving us
from evil. *Allahu akbar! wakul rabbi zidni ilman!"*

Then Saif strode with measured step, preceded by drums,
balafos, tom-toms, lambis, and trumpets, and his sorcerers sang
that he was invulnerable. His guard carried long bulls' tails
which, so it was said, diverted bullets. Kratonga, Wampoulo,
and Yafolè, covered with fetishes and carrying roosters, walked
behind His Royal Magnificence with Madoubo, murmuring sac-
rificial prayers.

And so the soldiers flocked to Mossé in clans to fight the
Germans; in advance of each tribe went its sorcerers, bearing on
their arms and skulls the emblems of their superstitions. They

chewed "sublimated" tobacco, prepared by the Great Spirit, and their guns too, assurance was given, were talismans. So be it. Let us pray the Master of the Worlds for good health and protection here below and in the other world. *Allanéou.*

And the tradition says:

"Man, lower your voice. Do you not know that His Royal Magnificence Saif ben Isaac al-Heit is everywhere present to those who do not recite his praises?"

And accordingly:

How in the face of the troops fanaticized by Saif the Germans retreated stubbornly and bravely to the towns of Ruande and Gnoundere, where their resistance was broken only in 1916 by the Franco-British troops under Generals Dobell and Aymerich; why the military cemeteries that still line the road cut through the jungle between Buanda Fele and Ruande bear witness to the fury and obstinacy of a hopeless struggle; how Taruatt surrendered in June 1915, Gnoundere shortly afterward, and Ruande in January 1916; how at Zora, far to the east of Nakem, the last outpost of Fousséri, Major von Rabben was besieged for more than eighteen months and surrendered only when news came that Governor Ebermayer had evacuated the territory; why he was decorated for heroism; how Colonel Zimmermann succeeded in breaching the French lines in South Nakem and escaped to Spanish Guinea with the wreckage of his army; why in this merciless war the armed enemy was often less dangerous than the jungle, the fevers, the climate, and the isolation—all these are matters which there would be little point in developing.

Throughout this period Abbé Henry—the hunchback priest obsessed by the tragedy of the Blacks, half crazed with the Christian duty of love, as humbly beautiful as the despair of a Christian soul—had been going from village to village, from hut to hut, a worker-priest even then, hoeing the peasants' fields, caring for the sick, providing medicines, and when night came reading the Acts of the Apostles.

During the four years of war, years of frenzy and horror, of pitiful joys and death-dealing laughter, he sowed the gospel of the sweet Lord Jesus among the natives huddled in terror as the shells burst roundabout, while not far away in festive procession the notables hailed the glorious violence and sang the praises of Saif the invulnerable.

The cannonade had set fire to the forest, a bloodstained dawn illumined the sky and the gray huts.

For the first time in Africa a dense layer of smoke produced by human madness all but blotted out the radiant April sun. For almost ten miles around Tillabéri-Bentia all was apocalyptic darkness.

Indefatigably, tearing himself away from loudly lamenting families, Henry helped the people, begging his sustenance on the roads and trails of Nakem. At Krebbi-Katsena he collected medicines, bandage, the old clothes of colonials or *tirailleurs,* loaded them on a donkey and brought them to the hamlets that had suffered most from the war.

He held out his hand to soldiers on the trails, genuflected as he approached peasants, or, standing motionless at the edge of a field, arranged to work for a pittance; and his face was so weary, his humped body so striking, that alms were never refused him

The poor man gave whatever he received to widows and orphans, ground millet for his elders, and occasionally replaced a sick or repatriated teacher at one of the mission schools.

One night at the village council in Toula, humility bade him say that he had let Sankolo die and had killed Barou, who had come to him to confess; they all thought he was mad and, swearing by Saif, ran away from him. In hamlets where he was known, the children fled at the sight of him to their mothers, who slammed the doors of their huts and showered him with imprecations. The gentler souls left a bowl of millet at their doors, went inside, and drew the latch.

Rebuffed on all sides, he went on bringing medicines, though no native would accept them; he lived on yams, roots, windfall fruit, and soldiers' leftovers. He seldom showed his face in the villages.

Then one of the sons of Savadogo, the Toula village chief, fell sick. The sorcerers brought herbs, the magi laid on hands, the notables prayed—to no avail. The child was stricken with yaws: Henry saved him by the proper aseptic treatment, and the wall of antipathy around him crumbled.

Pouring in from the outskirts amidst stray sheep hung with amulets, amidst dizzily striped cotton prints offering their naïve designs—palm trees, portraits of Saif, masks, rhinoceroses, ships—to the wind, the street crowd, among them the friends and relatives of the sick, drove before them, stumbling over the stones, splashing through stagnant ditchwater, a throng of men, women, and children, red-eyed noseless lepers, yellow-spotted lepers covered with scabs and pus, who stretched out their black, fingerless, pink-splotched hands to Henry. Some held out meager scrapings of food in earthenware pots also used for feeding ducks; there were sufferers from smallpox chewing *dabali,* their lips swollen from the drug; here and there a member of the crowd took fright and tried to slip away; enormous thick-lipped black women with amber rings in their ears, a noble melancholy in their faces, and no other covering than tattered loincloths muttered that they were sick with syphilis; others flung themselves slavering at Henry's feet, screaming that they had been bewitched by sorcerers or threatened with death from a distance; consumptives coughed blandishments at Henry, tried to speak, spat blood, and tried again to force the barrier of words.

Henry made himself a hair shirt with iron spikes. On his knees he entered every house with more than four grain lofts: houses of notable polygamy. Here he obtained food and clothing, dressed the ragged and fed the starving. He washed the feet of the disinherited folk, whose skin, covered with scaly pustules, was colder than a snake and as rough as a file.

Then he loaded his patients on mules donated by the rich, stopped at infirmaries where he gave them first aid, and set out for the hospital at Krebbi-Katsena. His face was so ravaged, he looked so haggard, that his helpers could not contain their pity. They prayed and wept as they made their way piously amidst the terror sowed by the war.

They spent the night packed into an abandoned hut, in a pestilential vapor as dense as fog; more vigilant than ever, Henry shared their couch. Saif, who received his subsidy irregularly because of the war, had got into the habit of selling porters as slaves and sending them to Khartoum, Zanzibar, and the Arab world. A number of his acolytes, who preached *habbo*\* against the English and French, were using the Libyan desert, inadequately policed by the Italians who controlled the coast, as an infiltration corridor.

But human conflicts have consequences that are at first scarcely discernible; in the perspective of history we see them clearly.

This is what happened:

"By the Treaty of Paris of September 8, 1919, and the London Agreement," the chronicle relates, "nearly the whole of eastern Nakem, beginning at Fousséri, was ceded to England, while France acquired a hundred and fifty miles of new frontiers. Thus Ziuko—including Taria and Souia in the South and Riboa in the North—was to round out the definitive frontiers of the future African republic of Nakem-Ziuko."

From that time on, the Gonda, Fulani, Ngodo, Mandingo, and Zobo school children, in addition to singing the "Marseillaise" (so be it), have been studiously commemorating the assassination of Jean Jaurès (may the Lord have mercy on him), the Marne (praise be!), Verdun (the Eternal), Europe in flames (upon it salvation), the Italian defeat at Caporetto (amen), the retreat, the victory (glory to the Most-High), and thirteen million dead (may the Lord refresh their couch), including the anonymous niggertrash dragged twenty thousand miles and fallen for unjustifiable ends. Forgive us, O Lord. May Thy holy protection save us from such calamity. *Amina yarabi.*

\* Holy war.

8

Amid the ruins of war poor Kassoumi daydreamed under his banana tree. His eyes roamed beyond the gray leaves of the budding fruit trees to the Yame River, foul with the stench of the carcasses and skeletons which fishermen had pulled out of the river in their nets—the decomposed corpse of some German in uniform, killed by a thrust of a lance or saber, his head crushed by a stone, or thrown from a bridge. The river muck buried these obscure acts of vengeance or heroism, these silent assaults more perilous than the battles fought in broad daylight and unheralded by fame.

Little by little his pious thoughts of former days, the stilled ardor of his early faith, returned to Kassoumi's heart. Education, which he had looked upon as a refuge from slavery, now seemed to him a noble livelihood that would save his children from the treacherous and painful existence that had been his.

In his desolation he thought of Henry, who had given the school children the habits of prayer and study. Instantly he rose and made his way to the darkened church across the Yame, where the pointed flame of an oil lamp, sacred guardian of the divine presence, glowed in the choir.

He confessed to Henry, confided his unhappiness, told him all his troubles. He asked him for advice, compassion, help, and on the following days he prayed repeatedly, with more and more fervor. Worn with trouble and anxiety, he was still intent on steeping his children in white culture and so helping them to grow up among Blacks. He had formed habits of increasing piety, learned to abandon himself to the secret communion, so comforting to the wretched of the earth, of the pious soul with the Saviour, and had received a great blessing in return, for Henry had accepted his five children at the French mission school: Anne-Kadidia, his lithe and graceful daughter, who bounded over the countryside like a rabbit; Raymond-Spartacus, the first-born, a squat little boy with a flat nose always covered with beads of sweat; Jean-sans-Terre, with the pious gait of a caged cat; René-Descartes, of the wide forehead; and René-Caillé, with lynx eyes and the look of a wild beast.

All the children wore amulets around their necks, except Kadidia, who wore hers around her waist. For the little girl school was a pleasant outing, alas too brief: she was dismissed the very first year; for René-Caillé it was a chance to swing from liana to liana; and for René-Descartes it was a kind of withdrawal (he lived in a daydream, in which he merely persevered on his school bench). Only for Raymond-Spartacus did study become a fanatical cult, the instrument of his emancipation; he was the most successful of the lot.

The lucky star that followed him all through his studies came, so it was said, from his amulet, which was not black like the others, but of red leather (the right of the eldest), bright as fire and possessing the virtue of philters: it might not resuscitate the dead, said Saïf, "but there is no wound or sickness which it cannot cure."

From morning till night Raymond-Spartacus fondled it in his little fingers, then raised it to his lips.

For many years, at the hour when night and day part, Tambira—her nails were as delicate as cricket wings—prepared food for her children, who seldom ate their fill in the servants' kitchen. They hardly had time to eat their bread before the platter was scraped bare.

"Don't worry, Mother," said the sons, "we'll go to school, we'll study to honor Father and you, and give you a happy old age."

Their father, Kassoumi, said to them: "Of course you'll go; what I'm afraid of is that you won't come back."

Heavy with sleep, the children ate at daybreak, then went back to bed and waited for the household to stir.

Or, armed with slings, they went down to the Yame at dawn and brought back a few turtledoves or partridges or wood pigeons, which Tambira wrapped in clay and baked in the coals.

Once the clay was cooked hard, she broke it; the bird's feathers came off with it, uncovering roasted flesh—and how succulent it was!

Dressed in a simple loincloth, the mother watched them eat; suns laughed on her face and moons sprouted on her breasts. But then it was time for school and Tambira rose from her stool and, seven times more beautiful than ever in her pride, accompanied her sons to the courtyard gate.

Their father Kassoumi followed her; they were as harmonious a pair as the sun and the moon in the sky.

So they lived for days, weeks, months, and years; but in 1920, on the last day of the dry season, Tambira, remembering that her sons were to take their final elementary school examination, was troubled and said:

"It's not right for me to sit here idle. I must go to Dougouli the sorcerer and offer up a sacrifice for the children's success."

Kassoumi was delighted: "If you have time, go ahead; it's not right for me to be sitting here idle either."

Her preparations made, Tambira pulled three of her silken hairs, threw them to the winds, then started for Dougouli's house, while her husband went out to the fields and the Yame.

Dougouli's house was across the river, half a mile from the Place des Flamboyants. Tambira was so absorbed that she didn't notice the man.

"For shame," said the sorcerer. "Don't you know me? I've prayed a whole year for the fruits of your womb to live." Then Tambira recognized Dougouli.

"Woman!" he cried in his shrill voice.

She looked at the sorcerer and saw in his face all the marks of religious frenzy. Her little black eyes expressed no indignation, she hadn't the right to be indignant; her lips twisted into a dazed, humble smile; and as though this sign of weakness had given the sorcerer every license, he began to squeal without restraint:

"By the Lord, Tambira, I know what brings you. Come in, be nice to Dougouli and win his favor."

They entered a dark hut lighted only by a little window in the slanting roof. The man's feeble mutterings filled the walls; she smiled humbly; he made little gestures demanding silence:

"O sun of suns and splendor of the sky, light of your family, beauty of the world! I've been expecting you for a long time. . . . What is your trouble? What has happened?"

"How should I not be troubled? My sons are taking their examinations to make me happy, and I haven't the strength to help them."

"Then I will help them," said Dougouli. "But on condition that you are good."

"Why wouldn't I be good when my sons have passed?" said Tambira.

Dougouli held out his right arm and instantly Tambira was spellbound. He struck the ground with the end of his amulet: from it arose a mortar full of grain and, wielding the pestle, a woman as powerful as a man, with the calves of a mountaineer.

"Hold out your hand, woman."

Tambira held out her hand and the sorcerer touched it: from it fell a dense rain that upset the mortar and emptied out its grain.

Dougouli struck the ground with the end of his amulet: a white lamb rose up with a look of startled innocence.

"Hold out your hand if you are a woman!"

Tambira held out her hand and the sorcerer touched it: from it arose six hyenas which chased the lamb and brought its torn carcass to Saif.

Dougouli struck the ground with the end of his amulet and a hundred serfs caught fire. He said to Tambira:

"You must save them."

"I'm too scared," the servant stammered. "You save them."

"Look," the sorcerer muttered.

He struck the ground with the end of his amulet and the faces of Tambira's sons appeared; petrified with ecstasy, the serfs bowed down, burst into song, and turned into white doves.

Miraculous water flowed to the ground from a calabash, and in it Tambira, hypnotized, saw her sons in the distance writing their examination papers. Praise be to God All-Powerful! *Aou-yo yéwa!*

"Sit down over there and take off your loincloth," the sorcerer commanded.

A hideous mixture of fear and revulsion rose to Tambira's throat. An animal, an animal worn out with mother love, she thought of her husband's love and unhappiness, and ignored the sorcerer's disquieting kisses on her neck, the gentleness of his caresses, the fire of his lips, the saliva of his mouth, the warmth of his dugs, his loins, his armpits, his belly, his glutted member, the quivering desire of his legs: she took off her loincloth and squatted in the puddle on the ground.

They looked at each other with eyes revulsed by desire; their lips were heavy and their hands trembled. Tambira's bare thighs were reflected in the puddle.

But now the sorcerer muttered prayers, traced signs, seemed to be listening to some distant murmurs, and suddenly, swollen with delirium, his lips spat out:

"Heh-heh! Look! Sitting there straight and motionless with your hairy pubis. Look! Red as the red of a cock's comb, it opens, yawns, dances, wiggles! Look! Heh-heh! What do you see?"

The puddle danced before the eyes of the spellbound Tambira, fascinated her drunken eyes, and bit them furiously; shapes whirled, plumed with violence and lust, in which her own shame shrank to insignificance. Suddenly a white cock arose from the puddle, then two white sheep with black heads; the cock crowed and the sheep bleated, then a whirlwind seized upon the puddle, lifted it up, sucked it in, and clogged its water with hundreds of feathers from the butchered cock and with the necks of the sacrificed sheep. Then nothing. Only the reflection of Tambira's gaping vagina, over the puddle. Then the puddle itself vanished, soaked up by the earth floor.

"Stand up, woman! Heh-heh! A white cock, weh! Two white sheep, heh-heh! Sacrificed to me, weh! And all your sons will pass," Dougouli prophesied.

Tambira pulled down her loincloth, sheathing her thighs. She was happy, but also terrified at the thought of the price: a cock and two sheep! . . .

"Before the morning star rises a month hence, happiness will come to you, Tambira, like a flock of swallows: a cock and two sheep, and your sons will pass. Unless . . ."

Her cry came from her heart, instinctive, spontaneous:

"Unless what?"

The sorcerer's eyes shot lightnings, and in spite of herself the servant felt hypnotized. The man wanted her. She loathed this sorcerer with his snake eyes, his heavy lips, his crooked legs, his wagging mule's head, his smell of blood and of amulets made from crudely tanned leather. Resolutely she closed her eyes, and the fascination vanished. She was free of it as long as she avoided the man's eyes.

"You will not go. The cock and the two sheep, or yourself right away. No. You first. Then we shall see."

He closed the window and approached the woman. A slap in the face stopped him.

"Woe to your household!" the sorcerer yelped. "Maybe I won't hold your belly to my loins in this world, Tambira, but when your children are dead—crooked be your path!—how will you escape me?"

Then, brimming with anger but fearing the sorcerer's occult vengeance as much as his black magic, the woman whimpered like a faithful dog, lay down on the ground and undid her loin-cloth.

When she left the hut with head low and shoulders high, Kratonga and Wampoulo were waiting. They had followed her and there they were. Threatening to tell her husband. They too had vengeance in their grasp: years before, Kassoumi had informed on the murderer Sankolo (their friend).

They bade Tambira follow them, and she obeyed. Impelled by an abject, cowardly fear, fear of her husband, such a good man and now she had been unfaithful; and fear for him: they would have killed him; and perhaps for herself too.

Wampoulo and Kratonga dragged her to a grassy copse behind the Yame waterfalls. Both of them took her. All that day, by scaring her out of her wits, they took her and took her again, as often as they wanted.

Her head low and her shoulders high, she went back to the palace. All that night Kassoumi and his children waited for her. When she didn't come home, they looked for her, and again next day: in vain.

On the morning of the second day Kassoumi trembled when Wampoulo and Kratonga came for him.

Tambira's body had been found. In the back yard a latrine had been built for Saif's serfs. A rectangular pit full of feces swarming with caterpillars and worms of every shape and color, covered with planks on which the domestics huddled for their needs. The corpse had been found in the pit.

There she lay in a corner, fully dressed and set to rights, with worms in her nostrils; her head, held in place by a slipknot attached to one of the planks, emerged from the feces. In her right hand Tambira—suicide or murder?—held a cross that Henry had given her and her children's reader, awarded at the last commencement exercises.

The domestics were afraid to mention anyone, or to say anything whatsoever. In silence Kassoumi took a rope, moved the planks aside without disgust, pulled out the oozing body of his beloved, and washed it tenderly. Now and then, while washing it, he sucked the nose and spat out a worm. He made no complaint; resigned, without even the strength to weep, he picked up the body with its dangling arms and, followed by the domestics in proces.sion, went down to his banana tree by the Yame, where one hot afternoon he had seen her for the first time. There he buried her. She had the love of her family. May the Most-High snatch her up to Heaven! *Amina yarabi!*

And the sky turns blood-red as we kneel down and the evening prayer arises:

In June 1920, all the sons of Kassoumi and Tambira passed their final examinations.

"Come, my sons, don't despair," sobbed Kassoumi, his eyes full of tears. "The days of mourning will pass. The Lord is present, He watches over your souls; study, my gentle lambs, study. Peace and happiness upon you. May the milk that fed you be profitable to you. And you, Raymond, the first-born become so brilliant and good that the mere sight of you will change the black night within us into bright day—may your success gleam like a sword and be more penetrating than an arrow. I have spoken."

And so the sons studied and the father attended to his servile occupations. But one day Raymond came home in tears and threw himself on his chair so furiously that its four legs broke.

"What has happened, my son?" his father asked. "Have you been insulted? Are you sick, or have you been expelled from school?"

"Oh, it's a hard life to study and to be a motherless child. All day long Rokia's boy made fun of me for not having a mother and being first in class; he shot at me with his sling, he wouldn't even let me speak, and they were all—a lot of dunces—on his side. How can I go to school after such an affront?"

"Calm yourself, O my sorrow; what did he say, my joy?" Kassoumi asked.

*"Dog and son of a dog, whose mother died in the serfs' latrine! The milk is still dripping from your mouth and you think you can measure up to me? Eh, you accursed perjurer, stick to your own people.* Oh, Father, how can I show my face now?"

"Such contempt is a matter of two days, and our shame is not so great. I'll tell you a way to make them forget it. Mount my donkey wrong side forward, your back turned toward its head, and ride through the crowd of your comrades three times. Watch them closely, then come back and tell me what they do."

Raymond straddled his father's donkey wrong side forward and rode straight through the crowd of school children. All of them, big and little, solemn and mischievous, laughed till they were rolling on the ground.

He rode through again. No one laughed. "He must have some reason," they said, "for riding his father's donkey wrong side forward; there's some good idea behind it. . . ."

When Raymond came home, his father asked him gently: "What did they do?"

"The first time I rode through, they laughed so hard they rolled on the ground. The second time, a few laughed but the rest didn't, and more than one was dismayed to see that I, the model pupil, had lost my wits. The third time nobody laughed. 'He's not crazy,' they said. 'He's not riding his father's donkey wrong side forward for nothing: he must have some idea. . . .' "

"Well, that's how it will be with the whole affair," said Kassoumi. "First they'll laugh, then they'll be dismayed, and then they'll forget all about it."

And indeed, when Raymond's schoolmates saw that he was still the first in the class and that his father didn't remarry, they poked fun at first and then they forgot all about it. And the Kassoumi family was able to go on with its humble life. Praise be to God the Most-High. He is mighty in all things and can fulfill all our wishes. Let us revere Him: *Amina yarabi!*

On the strength of their elementary school certificates, the less gifted of Tambira's sons obtained lucrative employment as clerks in the administration at Krebbi-Katsena, where they were paid doubly, first by France, then by Saif.

Only Raymond continued on to the secondary certificate, which he obtained in 1924. From that time on, by Saif's order, he was exempted from household chores.

That year's vacation was the most terrible the boy had ever known.

His face gray and his big eyes as white as beaten sisal, he sat under his father's banana tree, impassive under the taunts of the ragamuffins who shouted at him from a distance, calling him a lazybones. To tell the truth, most of the serfs had never welcomed his success, for in the fields pen pushers are regarded as bringers of harm, and the peasants would gladly have done as chickens do, killing the sickly among them.

Leaving the Yame, Raymond sat down at Saif's door, as still as the date palm in the courtyard. He didn't move, he didn't stir; only his eyelids, shaken by nervous suffering, dropped now and then over the white spots of his eyes. Did he have an idea, a clear consciousness of his life, drawn as it was between native and French ways?

This went on for some weeks. But in the end his helplessness and impassivity exasperated Saif's serfs. He became their whipping boy, their martyr and clown, a prey to the native savagery and drunkenness of the brutes who surrounded him.

Kratonga thought up all manner of cruel jokes inspired by Raymond's diplomas. And because he ate with a fork and dressed like the Whites, his meals became a circus. The serfs of the neighboring houses came to look on; word was passed from door to door, and every day the kitchen of Saif's domestics was full. Sometimes they put a puppy on a stool close to the mahogany bowl out of which Raymond was eating his millet. The animal smelled the food and approached very slowly, stealing a mouthful and barely escaping the thrust of Raymond's fork Crowded against the smoking walls of the kitchen, the onlookers laughed and wriggled and stamped. Raymond's father was never there—Kratonga had sent him on some errand to the other end of town. And without a word Raymond resumed eating, handling his fork with elegance and smacking the yelping puppy with his left hand.

On other occasions they told him Saif wanted him; when the young man tried to get up, someone tripped him and he fell against the sooty kettles.

Then they wearied even of these distractions. Furious that Raymond's education promised him a life better than his own, Wampoulo beat him and slapped him, laughing with the others at Raymond's helpless efforts to ward off the blows and return them. A new game was invented: the game of the eyelids. The servants, men and women, would thrust their hands in his face, and his eyelids would blink convulsively. He didn't know where to turn and always held his arms up to ward off the approach of those black savages who bellowed when they spoke to him, laughed like jackals, and reveled in his answers. Staring him straight in the eye, they invented his love life, saying that he was promised to Tata, a stout, plump-cheeked girl who carried great platters of food in her fists and whose eyes filled with tears at the sight of the torment inflicted on Raymond.

Soon Kadidia returned from the market, where she had gone to sell faggots, and stammered at the servants: *"Yourou mendè.* Have pity, for God's sake!"

All hung their heads, said they were only teasing her brother, and subduing their hatred went back to their lowly chores with a joke or two at Tata's expense.

They were not mistaken. Tata seemed to awaken all the faculties of tenderness that had lain dormant beneath the misery of Raymond's servile condition. For hours she followed him from afar down the long gravel walk that traversed Tillabéri-Bentia from the Place aux Acacias to the Yame. She watched him walking sadly, his hands behind his back, his head bowed. Sometimes he stopped, turned around, and smiled at her, as though he understood—and thanked her for feeling things beyond her years.

In the end they sat down in the pale-green millet fields along the river, for the girl would never have crossed the dividing line to which she had grown accustomed. Her vision was blocked off by a line of trees, and she had no idea whether or not the world extended beyond it. She chatted with Raymond. When after the midday meal the serfs, sick of seeing them always at the edge of their field, cried out to them: *"Han! yérago pili bara!* Why don't you go to the Flencessi with your white nigger instead of hanging around here? *bédéguéi gombo oumo héyé hein!"*—she made no answer but went away from Raymond, seized with a vague fear of the unknown, of the schoolboy's "culture," of new faces, the Whites, the suspicious looks of people who didn't know her; and instinctively, when she caught sight of the gendarmes who two by two patrol the road to Krebbi-Katsena, she hid in the bushes or behind a pile of stones.

Seeing them in the distance, booted, white and resplendent in the sun, she suddenly recaptured a strange animal agility and darted to some hiding place. She crumpled like a doll, rolled up into a ball and tumbled down the slope, becoming smaller and smaller, till she was no more visible than a hare in its burrow, her brown rags indistinguishable from the earth. Not that she had ever had any dealings with the police; but the fear of them was in her blood, inherited no doubt from her parents who had died at forced labor, working for the colonials.

Encouraged by Saif, Raymond became engaged to her. *Oum ibem min imbè: ama yéguéré!*

One morning in August 1924, in the midst of the rainy season, Saif was summoned to Mossé; returning at noon, he announced to the Assembly of Notables that Raymond Kassoumi had been authorized to pursue his studies in Paris and would leave in a month's time so as to be there for the opening of the school year. Saif, who regarded him as his property by virtue of his birth, his education, his heredity, his future, and as an instrument of his own future policy, heaped him with favors and saw to it that the serfs treated him with respect. Indeed, he was so pleased that, opening wide his palm without fear of exhausting his bottomless resources, he married Raymond's brothers to the servants of the learned Moses ben Bez Tubawi and showered his father with presents: *wassalam!* He made Raymond his favorite and, wishing to provide a special attraction at the forthcoming festivities, he ordered, on the strength of his ancestors' merits— may Allah honor their faces!—a *tchiprigol,* a contest of wrestlers—his serfs—in an arena of sand covered with millet straw, corn husks, and kapok, in the left-hand corner of the palace courtyard.

At his command two naked men appeared—Tukulör Blacks —bull's hide jock straps, hands armed with panther claws. They attacked at once, determined to lay each other low, clawing bloody stripes into each other's flesh.

Quivering, eyes wide in a vacant stare, the two wrestlers stood facing each other on firmly planted legs. Then suddenly they clashed. A body lifted high wrapped itself around the lifter's torso. Then like a great living weather vane it swung around his head, until with a sudden knee pressure in the neck it brought the lifter down like a lump of soft dough. The onlookers waved their legs in the air, jumped for joy, grunted with delight, and quite unconsciously imitated the movements of the wrestlers. Amidst their ferocious, delirious cheers the battle resumed, more desperate than ever. Both men were a mass of open wounds, the sharp claws dug into their flesh like rakes. The smaller man's cheek was in tatters and the other's ear, a bloody flag planted in his skull, was split into three pieces.

"Hit him, what you waiting for? *karmadjo! warmo!*" shouted the furious crowd. The larger fell unconscious and was carried away amidst a general ovation and exultant howls:

*"Naguè! naguè! hockèmo naguè!* A cow to the winner!"

Then with a long sigh of regret, sorely grieved that the end had come so soon, the onlookers went home.

The life that Raymond lived from that day on was the life of his whole generation—the first generation of native administrators maintained by the notables in a state of gilded prostitution —rare merchandise, dark genius maneuvered behind the scenes and hurled into the tempests of colonial politics amidst the hot smell of festivities and machinations—ambiguous balancing acts in which the master turned the slave into the first of the slaves and the arrogant equal of the white master, and in which the slave thought himself master of the master, who himself had fallen to the level of the first of the slaves. . . .

The engagement of Raymond and Tata was made official, designed to bring the half-whitened nigger back to Saif from France. For he was enamored of his betrothed, a big, stout, fat, ripe woman but very beautiful, with a heavy, hot, powerful beauty that caused men to dream and smile, and made her mysteriously desirable. A burgeoning of life in radiant happiness— interrupted by the student's departure.

A large crowd saw him to his boat, which wheezed and trembled like a kettle: his relatives, his fiancée, Saif and the Assembly of Notables, Kratonga, Wampoulo, Yafolè, Henry, beggars in turbans that had as many holes as a grain sieve, and a sprinkling of government clerks. And then the separation: a blaring of whistles, and the ship moved away from the dock with its medley of cottons and silks, its dashikis and old loincloths. Songs in praise of Saif, shouts of advice and admonition, smiles and tears, and the frail voices of children trotting like a brood of black chicks around their solemn parents. *Djoulè: homoh andi djitingal? djoulè! Amina yarabi* . . .

<h1 style="text-align:center">9</h1>

But it was too soon and too late. Smitten by Europe, a second shadow of himself, Raymond had already known Saif's fevers.

The white man had crept into him and this white presence determined even the moves that he, a child of violence, would make against it. Despising Africa, he took giant strides to diminish the gulf that separated him from the splendors of white civilization. But a simultaneous grasp of twenty centuries of history, or of their residue, was still beyond his reach: where he should have discovered—may the Evil One be banished!—he accepted.

And so, taking refuge beneath the dead tree of academic complacency, a mage of knowledge without hearth or home, living amidst the dead carcasses of words, Raymond Kassoumi, after a period of apery in which he took on the accent of a Paris wise guy, gave himself up to literary drivel, turning his learning into a demagogic ventriloquism and sinking under its weight.

Months of failure, of inadaptation, of confusion, of bumbling mechanical recitation, of flamboyant letters in which he justified himself to Saif: he could no more rid himself of Africa than a plant of its roots.

But France fascinated him, his teachers, his classmates, the white man in general, how different from those of Nakem, monosyllabic gendarmes the whole lot of them, except Henry.

Tambira's son was obliged to repeat his last year of school; he was humiliated to find himself by far the oldest in his class at the

Lycée Victor-Hugo, yet all the while he marveled at the distant, continuous rumbling of the belly of Paris, its women, those lithe blondes, brunettes, and redheads who passed by the gate of the students' dormitory, displaying the double provocation of their fine-grained throats and their bouncing buttocks, so close to him with their red lips and engaging eyes, spraying his desire with the smell of their powder and perfume. . . .

His life ran on, a sedentary life as dismal as the winter, which was long and hard. Then the first spring brought new life to the lycée; the students worked like laborious ants, reviewing for hours, toiling in isolated corners of the study halls under the lash of their ambitions, clutching books of all shapes and sizes which engendered knowledge in the candidates and wonder in their parents who, admitted by the supervisor, were waiting in the reception room to encourage their children, those larvae of culture.

The year was beginning well, so said the teachers, those purveyors of language confirmed more than ever in their importance by the febrility of their advice, of the homework and drill they imposed, the bric-a-brac of intellectual devotion which allowed them to shed temporarily the anxieties of that proletariat of the mind, the teaching profession.

They listened to their students as a conductor listens to his musicians. Striking the desk with an abject ruler: "Monsieur Bertrand, Monsieur Bertrand, that is a solecism! What is the function of $x$, Monsieur Kassoumi? One must grasp the spirit of the language, boys. . . ."

The concert had not been wasted. For suddenly, a month after the examinations, a great cry of joy went up; the young men swore, howled, coughed, and spat out their projects for the future, speaking of the contents of their examination papers as the son of a painter or poet might, at the age of ten or twelve, speak of painting or poetry; all, including Kassoumi, had passed, they were all *bacheliers,* except for three provincials from Charente, who looked like shepherds.

Cabling to Henry and Saif, Raymond felt justified in the eyes of Nakem, the lycée, and himself after so many months of a silence when, thinking himself lost, his career broken, he had forgotten even his family. Drunk with success, he arranged with a few classmates to go out somewhere for a good time after dinner that same evening.

Night was falling. In Pigalle the lights were going on. Six classmates set out slowly and hesitantly, in a procession two by two, through the warm Saturday evening.

Burning with the hunger for women that had fired their brains for the last month, they passed through the narrow streets bordered by cheap hotels. Pierre Duval and Philippe Bourdeau were in the lead, guided by Lamotte, known as "Dédé Bamboozalem," an intelligent scamp, hard-working and shrewd, who played the part of negotiator whenever a girl called out to them. He guessed which ones were whores, went up to them, and bargained with his fly half open like the curtain over a bar door.

After sauntering through nearly all the streets on the hill above Place Blanche, Dédé chose a steep alley full of neon signs indicating the names of night spots, sonorous colorful names blinking in the darkness. . . . On the sidewalk women resembling policemen in aprons were selling French fries; at the sight of the passers-by they stood up and hailed them, offering their three-day-old wares.

Here and there posters displayed naked women, whose qualities were touted by doormen in uniform; and farther on, behind a glass door, a swarm of smiling girls could be seen, displaying great pink breasts under some gaudy pretense of a covering and thighs of varying caliber. In another doorway stood a woman in green silk; the roundness of her body contrasted with the skinniness of her long red face, surmounted by a blond chignon framed in long strands of hair that hung down over her temples like thick side whiskers—a living sandwich, two cushions of hair compressing a slice of ham cut into the shape of a human head. This creature, an old toad huddling in an uncomfortable niche, called out to them: "Come on, kids, get yourselves sucked!" She came out and fastened on to Kassoumi, calling him her honeypie, stroking the back of his neck, cajoling him in word and gesture with all the energy of a ruined, indebted, avaricious woman, clinging to him as a usurer clings to his debtor. Bewildered and conscious of being the only Black in the group, Raymond resisted feebly while his comrades, watching him, hesitated whether to ask the price or pursue their bawdy adventures somewhere else. When the woman began to be annoyed and annoying, Dédé, who knew Pigalle, gave the marching order.

And they sauntered off, pursued by the enraged woman's vituperations, while other women, tapping on the glass doors of every hotel they passed, shot glances full of promise at them. More and more aroused, they continued on their way between, on one side of the street, the cajoleries of the gatekeepers of love and on the other side the oldest insults that have ever been flung at the human body. Now and then a group passed in the opposite direction—soldiers, sailors, hardened bachelors, vice-ridden old men, beardless boys, or unregenerate family men—with a glitter of savage joy in their eyes.

On they went. Unknown passages opened before them, tortuous alleys where neon lights colored the gray pavement between walls dripping with the smell of women's flesh.

At length, with a wave of his hand, Dédé called a halt outside a high-class establishment not far from the Moulin Rouge.

It was an all-out orgy. Four months' savings were swallowed up. For the pleasure of egging each other on, they asked to be all in the same room, and for three hours, aroused to the bursting point, they kneaded, burrowed, and plowed their companions, whose mascaraed eyes seemed to shine perpetually with passion; there was something strange, something fiercely sensual in their parted lips, their teeth, even their smiles; and their firm elongated breasts as pointed as pears of flesh, as elastic as if they had had steel springs inside them, gave an animal quality to the caresses, reflected ad infinitum by the mirrors on the ceiling and in the four silk-upholstered walls, of these magnificent females, creatures of unregulated love.

All six in the same room, they lay quietly watching each other in the mirrors, then suddenly clutched their companions in desperate, howling embrace: gnashings of teeth, convulsions, and bites followed almost instantly by deathlike torpor. But after a while someone would sneeze or cough and all twelve would wake with a start, ready for new enlacements, their throats swollen with passion. The world seemed as simple to them as one and one is two, and in their minds a raucous moan took the place of thought.

Instinctively proud of their bodies, the girls did not hesitate to adopt, propose, demand, and vary the numerous positions that enhanced their inexhaustible riches: they placed themselves on their sides, on their backs, on the edge of the bed, on all fours; or else, legs in the air and knees parted, they bent backwards till their heads touched the floor and so, shaking with laughter, let themselves be taken; then their fingers strolled, ran, and gamboled over the boys' sensitive spots with a bold and knowing shamelessness. When at last they were glutted with love, exhausted with cries and movements, they nibbled biscuits and drank champagne, and after their strenuous embraces microscopic beads of sweat stood out on their bodies. And from their secret folds they gave off that smell of wild beast and sexuality that is the salt of copulation.

When all the bottles of champagne were empty, one of the girls went to the door, opened it a crack, and ordered six more bottles, three packages of biscuits, and some caviar.

Each man enlaced his companion—they changed partners frequently. They had moved the spacious and astonishingly high carved-wood beds together. And after another drink all around, the sextuple copulation, reflected by the wall mirrors, resumed on thoroughly rumpled sheets, while the shrill tones of a phonograph drifted in through the narrow window that opened out on the bar.

They stopped to eat and drink; then they started in again; then they ate and drank some more.

All were merrily tight. Each with his girl pressed to his side, the boys wailed, sang, and miaowed, threw kisses into space, funneled champagne down their throats, unleashed the human beast. In the midst of them Kassoumi was holding a plump and pretty black girl astraddle on his lap, gazing at her with eyes of passion. Less drunk than the rest, though he had consumed no less, he was invaded by other thoughts. A feeling of tenderness made him want to talk. Ideas would crop up, tease him a little, vanish, and come back in a swirling dance; he had something to say but he didn't know exactly what.

"Eh . . . eh . . . uh . . . you been here a long time? . . . er . . . eh . . . uh!"

"Two months," said the girl.

He seemed pleased with the answer, hummed a little tune, and tried another:

"You like what you're doing here? Er . . ."

For a time she said nothing. Then very softly:

"You get used to it. It's no worse than anything else. House-maid or whore. Doesn't make much difference, does it?"

He seemed sympathetic. Then abruptly: "You wouldn't be from Martinique?"

She said nothing but shook her head.

"Or were you born in France? . . . er . . . huh . . ."

Again she shook her head.

"Then you must be from far away?"

She nodded

"From where?"

She seemed to hesitate, to ponder, to make an effort. Then as though out of breath: "From Nakem-Ziuko."

He smiled again, delighted, and kissed her hungrily.

Then: "That's good, I'm mighty glad, er . . . er . . . huh . . ."

She in turn risked a question: "You a soldier?"

"No, sweetie, I'm a student."

"From far away?"

"Oh yes. I've come a long way, schools, exams, universities."

"You're lucky."

"Right. I'll need it to make a living."

Again she seemed tense and anxious, troubled by some fear. Then after a moment's silence, setting down her glass on the floor:

"Ever meet any students from Tillabéri-Bentia, by any chance?"

He slapped his thighs and writhed with laughter.

"Yes. Sure. Only today."

"Really? Honest and truly?"

"Honest and truly . . . er . . . er . . . or I wouldn't have said so."

"You're not pulling my leg?"

He raised his hand. "By my father's head!" he swore.

"Then do you know if Raymond-Spartacus Kassoumi is still studying?"

Sobered by the shock, he was seized with a sudden terror; but before replying he wanted to know more:

"Do you know him?"

Distrustful, she answered evasively: "Oh no, of course not. A guy has been asking for him."

"A white man?"

"No."

"Then who?"

"Somebody."

"From here?"

"No, from there."

"What do you mean by 'there'?"

"Oh, just a guy, somebody, somebody like me. Well, a woman."

"What does this woman want with him?"

"Search me."

They watched each other, ill at ease, suffocating with fear, dreading some terrible blow.

"Could I see this woman?" he asked.

"What would you tell her?"

"Well, I'd tell her . . . I'd tell her . . . that I've seen Raymond-Spartacus Kassoumi."

"Oh, I hope he wasn't cold."

"No."

"Or hungry. Was he doing all right with his studies?"

"Oh yes. Yes."

Again she fell silent, evading his eyes, thinking what to say.

"Where are the students from Tillabéri-Bentia?"

"In Paris, of course."

She was unable to stifle a feeble cry: "What!"

"Why, yes."

"Do you know him? Do you know Raymond-Spartacus Kassoumi?"

"I've told you I know him."

Staring into space, toying with her heavily fingermarked champagne glass, she hesitated. Then: "Listen. Tell him . . . no, never mind."

Tortured by fear, he gaped at her. Finally, determined to get at the truth: "Well, what do you want of him?"

"Me? Nothing. I swear . . ."

Then, suddenly making up her mind, she crossed the room naked, picked up the young man's clothes as well as her own dress, and came back: "Put these on."

"Why? I've paid."

"Put them on, I tell you. Then I'll talk to you."

Obediently he dressed, watched her fit her brassière over her splendid breasts and slip into her dress. When she had finished, she sat down. The others had resumed their caresses.

"All right, I'm listening."

"First swear you won't tell him you saw me. You won't tell him, will you? And you won't tell him I'm a whore? Promise."

"I promise."

"By your father?"

"By my father."

"All right. You'll tell him that Tata, his fiancée, is dead—Saif accused her of knowing too much and refusing to play the game with Raymond—that his father was sold and shipped south to Dalbard with three hundred serfs, that Saif drugged two of his brothers, Jean and René, because they were government clerks and wouldn't do what the notables told them, and they went mad two years ago."

He felt dizzy, as though air were churning through the lobes of his brains. For a moment he was too stunned to speak. Then suddenly incredulous: "That's a lot of nonsense."

"It's the truth."

"Who told you?"

She put her right hand on his head and looking him straight in the eye: "Swear you won't tell anybody."

"I swear."

"I'm his sister."

"Kadidia?" he cried out.

She watched him again out of great round eyes, fixed with terror, and whispered haltingly through the fingers she had placed on her lips:

"What? What? . . . Is it you, Raymond?"

They sat there motionless, their eyes riveted to one another. Around them the ten others wailed softly. The sound of their flanks, the coming and going of their bodies, the cadence of their breathing, the raucous tumult of their embraces mingled with the squeaking of the phonograph. She was sitting there beside him, he had possessed her, he had been drunk with her body as she with his, brother and sister. And very softly, for fear one of his friends should overhear him, Kassoumi moaned:

"Oh God! Oh God! Oh God! . . ."

For a moment her eyes were clouded with remorse, and she stammered: "It's my fault, isn't it?"

But Kassoumi said brusquely: "So she's dead, they've been drugged, and he's been sold!"

"Yes."

"My fiancée, our brothers, our father!"

"All four in three months. During the rainy season. I was left alone, with nothing but my shift and my loincloth. I ran away and followed our father from the distance. He didn't want me to go, he was afraid for my sake.

"I went to work as a servant for Jean-Luc Dalbard, the French dealer in rare wood, well, that's one of his businesses. Father worked there for six months without wages. Dalbard was supplied with *dabali* by Saif and Tal Idriss. He mixed all sorts of stuff in the food to give the workers a hard on, so the poor bastards would work their balls off for more drugs and women—Wampoulo supplied most of the women. When the census takers were coming, those crooks would send their workers back and forth, to each other or to somebody else who bundled them off to Mecca. A pilgrimage, they called it. But you see, the notables came back from those phony pilgrimages, the drugged workers didn't. Hell no. They'd been sold and resold.

"And then one morning I got up. Father's not at work. They'd been flogging him till he was half dead because he'd always refused to touch those women. I knew he'd run away. He hadn't wanted to take me with him . . . maybe they killed him. Or caught him and brought him back. I don't know. I went down farther south and another white man, Polin, a druggist, seduced me. We're so dumb, you know. Then I went to work as a maid for an old coffee planter; he went to work on me and put me in a pad in Grosso, because he'd got me pregnant. After a while he stopped coming around; for four days I had nothing to eat, I couldn't work any more, so I started whoring like a lot of other girls. The next month I lost my baby. I've come a long way too, I've seen a lot of places! Africa, the ocean, Tangiers, Gibraltar, Toulon, Marseilles, Le Havre, Paris, and here I am!"

The tears flowed from her eyes and nose, ran down over her cheeks and into her mouth.

"How could I recognize you?" he said. "You were so different, now you're so plump, so changed. But how come you didn't know me?"

"I see so many black soldiers," she said with a gesture of despair. "Besides, you're so big now, so different. . . ."

Crushed by a despair so helpless and so piercing that he wanted to eat his fists, he looked deep into her eyes. He was still holding her on his lap, clasping her head in his hands. After looking at her a long while he was suddenly struck by her resemblance to the Kadidia he had left behind in the old country, and to all those she had seen mad, dead, or sold. He drew her close and hugged her as one hugs a sister. His throat was clogged with long sickening sobs, the sobs of the defeated, and he stammered wildly:

"Kadidia! My little Kadidia! Here you are! Here you are!"

Then suddenly he stiffened, jumped to his feet, and started to bellow and to knock his head against the wall, smashing the mirror to bits. Then he took two steps and collapsed with his face to the floor. He writhed and cursed, pounded the floor with his body, his head, his teeth, and whimpered so pitifully that he seemed to be dying. The others looked on, the girls shrieking with laughter:

"The black boy is really plastered," said a blonde.

"We'd better put him to bed," said another. "If he shows his face outside, they'll take him away in the paddy wagon."

Kadidia paid for him and the madam provided a bed. Though hardly able to stand straight, his comrades hoisted him up to the maid's room, where his sister sat at his feet and wept with him until dawn.

A week later Raymond, taking advantage of Sunday to visit his sister, was told that a sadistic customer had concealed a razor blade in the soap on Kadidia's bidet and that in washing herself she had cut herself so deeply that the hemorrhage had drained her blood and killed her before help could come.

Kadidia's brother lived alone, all alone. He had little heart for study and barely scraped through his second baccalaureate examination. He spent two terms preparing for the competitive examinations for admission to the school of architecture. After several setbacks he had lost his scholarship, but he was so fascinated by his new life that he didn't worry very much.

He had resumed his old Tillabéri-Bentia habits, rising early, taking long walks, and eating whenever he happened to feel like it. Having refused to be repatriated, he lived by odd jobs, addressing hundreds of envelopes, trying his hand at bookkeeping, or working at night in the Central Food Market. But at the thought of his failure, of the dead or enslaved members of his family, or of Henry, who was still in Nakem, his heart began to pound. The next day he would drop his job and pick up some textbook, hoping perhaps to hit on the question that would "come up" at the next session.

When his pipe dream had evaporated, he arose from his wicker chair, sat down on his bed, and spent hours and days thinking about his misery. It was not so much anxiety as a nervous, physical need to nibble at himself, to kneel down to his narcissism, to glut and intoxicate himself with his despair. At length, goaded by hunger, he went out.

In the light of the street lamps he passed over the sidewalks which looked strangely moth-eaten with their blotches of rusty leaves; closing his eyes, with an effort at concentration as though exposed to a thousand eyes of invisible notables, he drank in the night, a long shudder that clung to his body, and gave his mind to the patterns of fate, endless questions that hid from view, then rose up in long corridors traversing the trees, the streets, the walls, and the silence roundabout, rising from the ground, falling from the leaves, crawling over his fears that rose up, took flight, crisscrossed, and vanished, returning in swirls, interlacing, and imperceptibly crumbling into a dense, dark, swarming human dust, only to return again as an obsession—which suddenly halted before his bastions of legend, God idle behind the hazy halo of his rising tears, amidst a smell of musty pavement.

When, singing the serfs' hymn of praise to Saif in the sadness of dusk, he was overwhelmed by weariness, his heart, like a rain of grief, a flood of despair, drove him to the crowds, the bustling sidewalks of the Latin Quarter.

He got into the habit of going to a café, where the drinkers around him, the dense pipe smoke, the thick beer, dulled his mind and quieted his heart.

He lived there. No sooner out of bed than he went looking for neighbors to occupy his eyes and thoughts.

"It's cowardice."

"Conviction."

"Cowardice," he repeated inwardly.

He battled with himself as he sat at *Chez François,* slowly smoking his cigarette, which gave him a good fifteen minutes of stupor. Then he leaned over his beer.

A trembling arose, first in his eyes, then passed like a tic over his nervous cheeks, parted his lips, dilated his nostrils, and opened his mouth; quickly his throat contracted, mingling the yellow liquid on his gums with saliva that spurted at the contact: a cascade of swift movements, a silent bird song, the last note of which would fall softly, warmly, fervently in his stomach.

To the harsh music of the phonograph, Kassoumi dozed, waking an hour later in midafternoon. He stretched out his hand to the beer that the waitress had set down while he slept; then, having drained it, he straightened his tie, smoothed the crease in his trousers, the sleeves of his jacket, and his shirt cuffs and pounced on the newspapers he had read the day before.

He read them through, headlines, notices, advertisements, comic strips, stock-market quotations, and theater programs. Between four and six he went to the Luxembourg Gardens, to take the air, as he put it; then, returning to the place that had been kept for him, he ordered his beer and chatted with the habitués whose acquaintance he had made. They commented on the political events, accidents, and disasters of the day. Then it was time for dinner. He tapped his glass with his saucer, and the waitress brought a plate, a glass, a napkin, and the menu.

When he had finished eating, he joined a group at the next table in conversation which made the evening follow in the traces of the afternoon. Soon it would be closing time. That was the moment he dreaded, when he would have to go back to his student's room and not study but be reminded of himself and his difficulties, as he had been every night for more than a year.

Kassoumi wanted to stay on to forget himself, but the place would be closing in half an hour and he couldn't make up his mind to reorder. With a mixture of pity, irritation, and contempt, the waitress, in an effort to make him leave, chided him for his nocturnal habits, his simple pleasures, his tastes, his looks, his gestures, the parsimony of his tips, and his placid tone of voice.

Kassoumi pretended not to listen. "All right, all right," he muttered, and headed for the toilet.

Once there, he pushed the bolt to be alone, thoroughly alone. He had become so accustomed to being treated rudely that he felt secure only when protected by locks. He no longer dared even to think, to meditate, to reason with himself, unless he had previously turned a key to guard himself against noise and recriminations.

Slumping down on the seat, he reflected that sooner or later he would have to do something about his finances; then perhaps he would be able to study with peace of mind.

The idea of immoral earnings frightened him, he didn't dwell on it. To work in a factory or as a day laborer was equally impossible. And in less than a month now his situation would be desperate.

He sat there with his arms dangling, casting about vaguely for some means to straighten things out. Finding nothing, he muttered: "Luckily, I've got a few degrees. . . . Without them I'd be in a real fix."

He thought of writing to Henry in Nakem and decided to do so; but remembering the hostility between the ecclesiastic and Saif, he was afraid the notables would regard him as a lackey of colonialism. And again he lost himself in his fears and uncertainties.

The waitress knocked at the door. He started. Someone was waiting and he hadn't even relieved himself. Frightened and harried, he sponged his forehead, buttoned up in haste as though summoned back to the café for important business. Then he strode serenely, frustrated but calm, glad to have nothing more to fear. He cast a glance at his newspapers, toyed with the oysters in the display of the corner vendor, and returned to his seat; but a door opened and the waitress approached.

In desperation he ordered another beer. Then suddenly the blood clamored in his temples sticky with heat and irritation, and he felt the eyes of someone in the street resting on him. He looked up.

The man was there looking at him; a middle-aged man with

an air of prosperous respectability, and graceful graying side whiskers, the points of which rested on his coat collar. He was smoking a cigar, watching Kassoumi as he sat behind his glass, following his every movement lovingly, seeming to dispatch kisses from the tips of his lips to Kassoumi's kinky hair, his eyes, cheeks, mouth, hands, then with a downward leap to Kassoumi's loins, where his attention concentrated with all the shamefaced tenderness of desire.

Surprised at first, Kassoumi started sipping his beer. He didn't take the man's behavior amiss, but was afraid of the waitress (who hadn't noticed the man's maneuvers) and dreaded the possible consequences. A moment's misunderstanding could bring disaster: vicious shrieks about homosexuality, insults flying between them like bullets and ricocheting through the room, cruel words that would make their hearts pound, parch their tongues, and leave them as weak as water.

The telephone rang. Someone—the manager—called: "It's for you, Gilberte."

The waitress picked up the phone. Her air of exasperation was gone, giving way to a cold, malignant determination that was even more frightening. Her phone call was brief. She came back to Kassoumi: "This isn't a flophouse," she said. "We're closing in fifteen minutes. You'll have to order something or get out. Take it or leave it."

She was waiting for an answer. Kassoumi stammered: "Yes, mademoiselle, of course."

"What'll it be?"

"The same."

She served him. He paid up and gave her a generous tip, his last centimes. It was midnight.

When she had gone, the stranger approached.

"Good evening," he said softly. "Nice weather we're having. Er . . . You don't mind?"

He pulled up a chair and in the same movement caressed the back of Kassoumi's head. The student slumped down in his chair and looked at the white man in bewilderment. He didn't understand; he felt stunned, stupefied, mad, as if he had fallen on his head; he scarcely remembered the horrible thoughts that had flashed through his mind for a second. Then little by little, like a muddy pool, his reason cleared, and abomination clutched at his heart. He, a nigger. What can you hope for if you're a nigger? The man had touched him, looked at him with such intensity, such assurance, such unabashed emotion that he could have no doubt, but persisted in doubting his own perspicacity, obstinately searching for those five seconds of complicity between them, trying, his memory sharpened by fear, to recapture each and every gesture. And each new discovery pierced his heart like the sting of a wasp.

Something strange and terrible was going on inside him, a cold pang, the memory of his misery, of his dead mother amidst the serfs' feces, a shudder in his limbs and his whole body, as though his bones had suddenly turned to ice. He raised his head and looked wild-eyed at the man; his thoughts wandered as though he were going mad; and under his gaze the man's face changed, took on weird shapes, absurd resemblances.

Kassoumi withheld his prayers. He had no choice. The man desired him. He had to live.

Questions quivered in his temples, the toppled forests of his blood bubbled, waves of nausea and gratitude traversed him under the man's insistent look, that salt as soothing as a balm and less hot than his breath. The student stood up: he had consented to sell himself.

His head was bursting, a desperate seed of virginal hope, a shattering of the world order. Leaning humbly on his shadow, victorious after many deaths, Kassoumi recognized in this tired portrait not so much a secret resemblance to himself as a silent meaning, an ineffable brotherhood of his being with the world's unhappiness in the face of its gigantic hunger for self-destruction.

"Come," murmured the white man. "Don't be afraid. I know what it is to be without a woman, what it is to believe in a woman, to belong to a woman and not to possess her, to suffer long silences, not to be a man with a woman, and then, instead of love, to know the silent cry of a thirst together. Come, come, my love, I've been looking for you a long time, in every body I ever encountered. Before I even knew you. Before I even knew the others. . . . A day freed from anguish by your love and mine—that's what I want. Just one day. Would you like that? A day that will save us both. You and me. You're strong and healthy. . . . You and me together, even if you know nothing about me. I'll teach you to make black sand out of love, our love, my sweet. Black body, I'm sick of having a stone under my head, I want peace—you will make me a pillow of peace. You alone can save me. You alone can destroy me. I want you to need me always, in the hour, in the minute, in the instant when I won't be there, but even so I'll inhabit the quiet warmth in which I hope to plunge your heart with my absence. I love you. Don't go away. I've suffered too much. My sorrows. I wish I could dissolve them in the bright light of your eyes. Come: I know at this moment, as I lay my outstretched hands on your arm, that you've never looked for anyone but me, oh my painful refuge charmed by my adoring caresses. Come. We'll soon be there. We shall gather drop by drop the light-sandaled dew that will still the storms within us, my sweet. Come, my garden."

They walked along under the street lamps, one behind the other as though impeded by some obscure fetter, zigzagging a little.

The wind murmured. The light sound caressed Kassoumi's ears, mingling with the man's words, which whirled about in his head, and then, as though exhausted, scattered into frescoes in which the silence wove another silence, a dream of peace and loving solitude. A moment of lull, in which their hearts filled with blood to the point of ecstasy. A rare sweetness bringing languor to their eyes. They walked on; their voices were low, colored by the sweetness of their despair and by their solitude clothed in all the richness of a single prolonged note, evoking with flawless beauty the delight, but also the inner fervor, of a shared death agony. They were under the hypnotic spell of a happiness which savors itself and discovers its uniqueness.

Suddenly they stopped. The man took a key from his pocket

and opened a door. He pressed a button. The light went on.

The apartment was comfortably, lavishly furnished. When Kassoumi had taken a bath, the man brought him something to eat. And soon they went to bed.

He made a remark or two about the quality of the light. Then silence. Both breathed whiffs of lethargy, which seeped into them, filled them with well-being. Time dissolved slowly into a mass of soft, melting, drunken sensations, a throbbing of their whole being. And above it the other's latent desire that a prayer might be answered by consent. Grazing the sheets as pale as a mirage, the white man's desire, through his half-closed eyes, drank in the shape which he sensed at his side. In his intoxication he smelled the warm vapors rising from Kassoumi's neck, his body, his loins. . . .

Kassoumi wanted to sleep.

He managed to keep his eyes closed for a long time. Imperceptibly the man imposed his presence. Kassoumi opened his eyes; the other surveyed the curve of Kassoumi's back. Diffusing a winged warmth over those blurred harmonies. Finally he propped himself up on his elbow. Kassoumi was dozing at his side. Half undressed. Their desire consumed the air they breathed. With his big toe the man grazed, then touched Kassoumi's heel, hesitated, stayed where it was, penciling light caresses on his skin . . . . Timidly he kissed his partner, whose mouth came to life and returned the kiss. They moved closer together.

The silky sheets rustled over their skin; astonished at finding a savor they knew in advance, they scarcely breathed; Kassoumi moved, and little by little found himself pressed against the whole length of the smooth body. Trembling with impatience, their bodies joined in a mute embrace; languid, feeble, and somehow cool, their hearts hovered in a dream as the minutes died away. . . .

They enveloped one another, pressing gently to feel each other the more; savoring in indolent weariness the cadenced rapture of their heartbeats. Soft moans, sighs of endearment rose to their throats; drunk with the scent and mossy softness of their hair, they forgot their senses. . . . From time to time a start, a convulsive movement illuminated their torpor, and they opened their eyes. Then peacefully the world faded and vanished. . . .

They were no longer man and man, lover and partner, but a creature apart, issued from some strange power of life, apogee of the natural order of love, a great sea that stretched out in a hammock and never spoke, but shuddered. Pressed together to the full length and breadth of their good, warm bodies, they breathed everlastingly the air stirred up by the sound of their pairing.

From time to time they exchanged a friendly word. And neither wearied of seeing the other's lips move, of seeing them part and work to express the thought that he too had never loved except to escape his own anguish.

At these moments a diffident tenderness aroused a surge of gratitude in both of them. Saying nothing, they took each other's hands and kissed each other at length. In slow sips Kassoumi, with the wretched look of a beaten dog, drank their fitfully whispered confessions of love, drank them with a gentle pressure of his tongue against his palate as he might have eaten flowers, airy-fingered roses. He loved this taste of rose petals when he kissed the man, relishing even the insipid taste of the air in his nostrils. And each breath seemed to carry an imperceptible train, the winnowing of harvests forever repeated: and what was born and what died, the sap that flowed, wrapped in the guilt of their two bodies, was he, Kassoumi, the son of a slave, the cornered, alienated nigger engaged in being reborn well-born. At the height of his effervescence he rose up to inhabit the long silence of this birth. He germed like the earth, and his anguish was an arid sand dune speaking to the parched winds, silently as in a rite; as if by its silence it wished to proclaim its solitude, to shout that it was serene, irrevocably itself, that it had never had any other desire than to be serene at the end of this second, at the end of this breath in him, at the end of himself. . . . And as though when they rested everything ended and ceased to move, the student breathed in the shudder of time, as long and slow as smooth silk against a cheek. . . .

The next day, under the weight of this quivering calm of his being, Kassoumi forgot how long he had slept. Pressed against the other, he sat bolt upright, as ineffably serene as his story up to that late hour when, asleep and knowing he was asleep, his thoughts melted into a single reverie, fading little by little into the lethargic dream of his will.

Inexplicably, pressed to the other, his hazy eyes on the other's body, he remembered school in Nakem, Europe shining resplendent over the whole earth, and heard the swell of the sea within him: he saw ships, he saw, through holes in the sky, slaves going to work, women being sold, children being flung into the water, priests, soldiers in armor, men in chains, oarsmen; he saw slave traders and their niggertrash, or, preserved forever amid the winds and smells of the world, the crimes of the notables and their sporadic cult of human dignity.

And then from the depths of forgetfulness faces and symbols rose up before him, at first dimly illumined, then diffusing into a fugitive, powdery smoke; gray ash fell on his eyelids, his misery appeared to him as a concrete familiar object followed by spinning shapes, a solemn, slow, and fecund dance, delirium, tumult, a welter of images, faces, lightnings, and cries rising to the surface of that muddy water in which his memory of famous names and places knew, recognized, and understood itself. Saif, Nakem, his own self, the pale face of this white man come from another world, a world so close at hand which he detested, appeared to him transfigured in the sudden lightning flash which illumined the long march of his memory back to the accursed land of his birth: and his search was not so much for ecstasy as for the profound meaning of his own destruction, the stain on his face suddenly splattered by his name: Spartacus!

Kassoumi knew the long wasting of his flesh, a wasting sprung from chaos, binding him and opposing him irremediably to the white man. When he kissed his lover with a hangdog tenderness, the house was calm and the sky blue, but the pale light of the sun set his inner eye on fire with the very mystery he was seeking to penetrate. He smiled at the other as usual. A little later he asked to be paid. *Alif lam!*

. . . He came back the next evening and the next, he came back for a week, three weeks, six months. And each time after their pairing he knew that once alone in his bath he would sit for long minutes immobile and bolt upright, horror-stricken, his eyes rigid under his half-closed lids.

As the other murmured words of love, he went on washing, no longer knowing who he was, where he was, no longer knowing for how long he had been staring distraught at the vast silent void of his anguish. . . . The next day his feet led him back to his own identity: fear, the problem of his body and his skin, the body and money of his partner, a shipwreck like himself.

Finally, on another afternoon of his despair, as he lay motionless, having closed his inner shutters to foil his consuming desire to see too much, he was invaded by a soft, buzzing dizziness and in that moment he knew how much he needed this white man, his warmth, his loneliness, how necessary it was for him to lose himself in his lover.

Lambert, who supported him from then on, was a man of ample independent means, the natural son of a Strasbourgeoise, the only woman, he owned to Kassoumi, whom he had ever desired. She troubled, fascinated, attracted, frightened, and aroused him—to him she was at once courtesan and virgin.

This man was the student's providence. Made for night life, indefatigable though he always looked exhausted, robust despite his pallor, elegant with his curled mustache, his graceful graying side whiskers, his light hair and delicate lips, he was one of those night people who derive an artificial nervous energy from gymnastics, fencing, golf, showers and sweat baths. A true Parisian, energetic and irresolute, indifferent and passionate, buffeted by contrary instincts and, masterful *bon vivant* that he was, inclining to all of them in pursuit of his private weather-vane logic, he let Kassoumi go on living in his room on Rue

Mouffetard, so enabling him to continue his studies, and in return for two nights a week gave him enough money for rent, food, clothing, and private tutoring.

Their affair lasted eighteen months. During that time Kassoumi squeezed through his examination for admission to the school of architecture. His scholarship was reinstated. And then disaster: Lambert's mother fell critically ill in Strasbourg and sent for her son. He flew to Strasbourg, followed by Kassoumi, who settled in a hotel room. There he worked up his first architectural projects and studied mathematics, statistics, mechanics, physics, the chemistry of building materials, construction, law, and art history: Lambert spent long hours at his mother's bedside.

She was slow to recover from her illness—decalcification of the spinal column. One day when Lambert came to his lover in the hotel room, he was rather flushed; there was a strange diffidence in his eyes; the irises seemed unnaturally blue and the pupils unnaturally black. He leaned against the door to recover his composure.

With an animal lust in his eyes and the curve of his lips, Kassoumi welcomed his lover. His bare throat rose and fell with his breathing.

"Sometimes," said Lambert with an air of embarrassment, "you look like a cat getting ready to lick my neck."

He sat down and the student followed suit. Lambert spoke of his mother and made ingratiating small talk in the charming voice that bewitched Kassoumi. Looking deep into Kassoumi's eyes, he seemed to be saying other words than those which came out of his mouth. Kassoumi pressed his lips to the first downy hair on the nape of his lover's neck, the spot he had long desired. Lambert shrank back a little; disgruntled at the feeling of inferiority that came over him, Raymond murmured:

"You've forgotten."

"What?"

"That I love you."

"The life suits you?"

"Stop joking. You know what I mean."

"Nonsense!"

"I do. I swear I do."

"What? I've forgotten."

"You've forgotten?"

"That's right."

"That's not what you said last night."

Lambert burst out laughing. Suddenly giving in to an obscure desire to get even, to avenge himself, to wound his nigger:

"My boy, I've decided to get married. My mother's arranged the whole thing. Even the announcements. Here they are."

They were sitting face to face, hanging on each other's eyes. For a few seconds Kassoumi remained motionless, as though reluctant to penetrate the meaning of the other's words. Then a tremor ran through his whole body. His face contracted from his chin to his forehead, his ears went purple, and he roared: "You hypocrite!" He threw his meager belongings, his clothes and books, into his suitcase and, overwhelmed, exasperated, frantic, left the room. He dashed down the stairs to the desk, in his hurry paid more than he owed, ran out into the street with the desperate haste of a man drowning himself in a river, and, under the bewildered eyes of Lambert, vanished into a cab.

For three years Kassoumi worked. Completing a competitive project each month, obtaining ten marks of distinction in each subject for a total of fifty "credits" (not to mention his outside work for architects), he became an "honor" student, a distinction never before attained by an African. He wrote papers the mere mention of which sufficed to give him, in Nakem-Ziuko, the halo of glory that is so flattering to the black imagination, which exalted him to a position above and outside of mankind. His compatriots came to revere him as a genius of science, culture, and intelligence. At the end of this period he presented his thesis.

There is little to be said of the obscure, unglamorous life he led in those years. Then suddenly, in 1933, the news that the thesis submitted by the "black pearl of French culture" had been accepted burst like a bombshell. At the same time, in defiance of all Saif's calculations, Kassoumi married a Frenchwoman, a girl he had first met in Strasbourg, whose mother, formerly a laundress, tended the dying in her neighborhood, sewing up her customers in steaming sheets which they were never to leave, then going off with her iron to smooth the undergarments of the living. As wrinkled as the rear end of a she-ass, loud-mouthed, hard-working, maniacally stingy, she yacked incessantly, sang popular songs at the top of her lungs, fought with the coal dealer, told the concierge that her daughter was going with "a nice colored boy with a future," and regaled the upstairs neighbor's maid with the downstairs neighbor's domestic secrets. Her head was chock-full of absurdities, of idiotic beliefs and grotesque opinions. Doubled over as if the everlasting movement of her iron had broken her back, she babbled on, as though moved by a kind of cynical love, about the death agonies she had witnessed.

According to the notables of Nakem-Ziuko—whom rumors of his new life had reached—what had attracted Kassoumi was his certainty that the society in which his mother-in-law moved was no better than an "advanced" nigger, living among Whites, was entitled to aspire to.

Madame Teyssedou, Suzanne's mother, had the spacious udders of a buffalo cow. She was stubborn and narrow-minded, the kind of woman who goes through life without ever suspecting any of its undercurrents, subtleties, or shadings, who perceives nothing and deforms everything, blind to the possibility that anyone might think, believe, or act differently from herself.

Mother and daughter lived next door to Kassoumi's room; he spoke to Suzanne, held her and had her, a big stout girl with ardent breasts and hips shaped like a lyre; his caresses explored the divine undulating line that runs from the throat to the feet, following all the curves of a flesh whose spirit, as simple as two and two is four, soon accepted him for husband before God and men. For six years Kassoumi lived in Strasbourg, working in various architects' offices, keeping up his payments on a house he had built for his mother-in-law and supporting his wife and three children, for Suzanne did not work.

In the end he was paid up and living the life of a middle-class white nigger. His only outside interests were Henry and a barmaid to whose heaving bosom he had recourse during his wife's lying-in periods.

No one suspected that war—that outburst of rage and grievance forever modulating the same litany—was near, that it would turn the world upside down and awaken nationalist demands in Tillabéri-Bentia the terrible, so shrewdly controlled by Saif. *Houlmoh! waar rèoudè!*

## 10

The nightmare now experienced by Raymond-Spartacus Kassoumi—*wallahi!*—was that of obscure millions, his contemporaries. When the shrieks of the cities terrorized by the murky light of bombs and rockets gave corpses the smell of eternity, many a man dreaded the invisible enemy as a sick cloud dreads the salt desert that it cannot cross without a caravan.

Soldiers fallen in the trenches—with flies on their lips and pus in their nostrils—or living to chew their despair of coming off alive, had rubbed shoulders with the unknown. With their absent muscles, spent eyes, voiceless throats, identical to this war they did not understand, which had plunged their heads into an all-destroying dream amid maddening confusion and the deafening music of the tanks. . . .

Flinging himself body and soul into the defense of invaded France with a by now unconscious impulse to protect the thing he loved, Kassoumi fought on the Rhine, at Cassino in Italy, and then in Provence.

Left for dead near Mehun-sur-Yèvre, where he had been buried under the ruins of a house, he managed with infinite pains to extricate himself. His face was swollen, his whole body ached. He waited until nightfall. Then, after his legs had struggled madly for three hours to keep up with each other, he found himself on a riverbank, under a willow tree surrounded by an enormous field of tender grass gleaming in the pale moonlight. He kneeled down, bent over, and drank the dark water; he let it flow slowly over his throat, an icy delicious caress—the shuddering of the light swift river which threw a dreamlike circle around the fleshless shadow of the trees. The Yèvre. The Yèvre. Mehun-sur-Yèvre. Where was he? Run. Walk. Get away. Hunger. No matter. Live. Run. Breathe. Survive. His gums. How was he to chew? His ankle. Keep on going all the same. The grass, the leaves on the trees, the blackberries amid the brambles, yes. Eat them. How was he to find his division? Suddenly a crossroads. He was on the road to Châteauroux. Sleep. Up there among the trees.

He woke up with a roar, choking a dim wriggling shape, a squirrel.

Cold shivers ran through him, his ragged nerves plunged him into hallucinations: unburdened of his limbs, he heard little rowboats every time he breathed.

Toward dawn he resumed his long march through the briars and nettles, reviewing the true moments of his life. When he forgot to hope, when he forgot to encourage himself, there came a silent hope that seemed to partake of death. He decided then to wait for the unforeseen. He too was a part of the landscape, something he could count on as he fell asleep in some dark thicket at the very moment when the world thought it could get him down by unfolding its rich assortment of dreams.

. . . He lived on leaves and wild fruit, on rats and roots; reduced to bestiality, he spent hours, nights, and months pounding his forehead with his fists to remind himself of the absurdity of attempting suicide. And that life, enigma of anxiety and fate, continued for eighteen months, which seemed to him a wide road shuttling between hope and death. And all the while, as he made his way through occupied France, he lived in terror of the Germans.

. . . When the narrow egoism of his fears left him, Kassoumi headed for a town, but no sooner had he reached the outskirts than, overcome with fear that some collaborator might denounce him, he hurried back to his thickets like an animal.

But in October 1945, sick and exhausted by the hardships of that fall—the previous winter, during which he had dressed in the skins of rabbits caught in snares, had undermined his health —he decided to make his way to Paris on foot, and to lose himself in the crowd. There perhaps he would be able to rustle up something to eat.

. . . His ears had long forgotten the sound of bombs and lamentations. In his grimy, tattered uniform he went to a bar in Orléans, represented himself as a sailor, and asked for work as a dishwasher. He was amazed at the quiet cheerfulness of the streets and faces. Filled with a passionate, painful love, a sick love weighed down by the memory of death, he heard the news, which came to him after so many nightmares, that Paris had been liberated on August 23.

He ran to the police station, described his long calvary, and gave them an account of his education and present state of misery. Notified immediately, his wife arrived from Strasbourg the next day. Two of his children had died, and so had his mother-in-law.

Suzanne found him at the bar, already established as dishwasher and hero. He knelt at her feet and she caressed his head with her fine fingers, murmuring words that tasted like the fresh water that flows in an oasis. And then Tambira's son learned of the vanity of his existence: his home in Strasbourg, along with the whole neighborhood, had been destroyed by the occupying power: Saif, the other, the bad white man, the Boche.

Born in an overseas colony, he was not a Frenchman; as Karim Ba, the interpreter, had written unctuously on his passport in Tillabéri-Bentia, Raymond-Spartacus Kassoumi remained a *French subject*. . . .

Orphaned by this world that had set on him a stamp incompatible with the usual conception of man, Suzanne's husband felt like a leprous witness, a groping blind man, a fanatic who kills with joy in order to assert himself.

He clamored to crush his misfortune, and driven by immoderate thirst he dwelt for hours on the vision of what his life, once

shorn of the unknown, might be. . . . And with delight his
tongue remembered the savor of Suzanne's lips. . . .

Meanwhile, in Nakem-Ziuko the winds of emancipation had
brought demands for reform.

Renard, the successor of Mossé, who had been transferred to
Indochina, had summoned Saif ben Isaac al-Heit to Krebbi-Katsena and informed him that Paris, wishing to associate the overseas populations more closely with the conduct of their own
affairs, left the natives free to choose their deputy.

Returning to his Assembly of Notables in Tillabéri-Bentia,
Saif explained to his dignitaries that the main concern of France
was not to be outdistanced by the headlong political development of its colonies. Now that the supra-national United Na-
tions Organization was coming into being, he pointed out, these
new progressive measures were essentially a translation, in legis-
lative terms, of the famous slogan coined at a time when France
was floundering in the bloody rice paddies of Indochina: "Let's
drop Asia and keep Africa!"

Accordingly, Saif dispatched Prince Madoubo to the traditional chiefs of the Nakem Empire and put pressure on them.
Harvesting the fruits of their policies of 1900, the notables pretended to co-operate with the Flencessi by putting forward those
products of French civilization, the sons of serfs, educated at the
Christian mission schools. Through them the Nakem traditionalists would not only govern but also defend their interests at the
National Assembly in Paris. *Amoul bop toubab, makoul fallè!*

Slowly, in the midst of debates, silences, and orders, the name
of a candidate cropped up, seemed to stick in men's throats—
and finally poured forth, sprung from the dark calculation of
some notable, not yet betrayed or even molested, but alerted.
Then suddenly this serene, friendly man grew alarmed. A free
man, restricted only by the uninhabitable desert of Saif's justice,
then from one moment to the next cornered, blocked on all
sides, he along with other dignitaries proposed to Saif hundreds
of half-whitened niggers, the sons of domestics: some, still wet

behind the ears, could hardly hold a pen; others, with no other distinction than an authorization to take the elementary school examination, proclaimed loudly that if they were nominated they would win at least twice as many votes as anyone expected; still others, graced with the title of "monitor of primary education," or "graduate," or even—miracle of miracles!—"*bachelier*," swore—yep!—that they'd never go home unless they were chosen as candidates.

The turbaned heads nodded, and each one in secret ruminated the same timid thought: the man of the hour was Raymond-Spartacus Kassoumi. His academic success in the land of the Flencessi had been bruited among the people, who declared that he was better educated than the best educated of white men— after God, by golly: *o djangui koié!*

Wasn't it true that in homage to his science a white woman had savored the ecstatic felicity of marrying Raymond the illustrious builder, who was far beyond the pretensions of any nigger woman, for—*tjok!*—he spouted mathematics and physics as easily as his mother had shelled peanuts. . . .

Definitely, hm, the man was no fool. O Lord, a tear for the niggertrash—have pity! . . .

More than one of Saif's councilors was aware that since the Shrobeniusologists, with their shrewd mixture of mercantilism and ideology, had watered at the mouth over the splendors of black civilization, and since the World Wars in which black soldiers had burst with violence in the service of France, a cult of the good nigger had arisen, a philistine Negromania without obligation or sanction, akin to those popular messianisms which appeal as much to the white soul enamored of niggerdom as Aunt Jemima's pancakes to the white mouth.

Under these circumstances the election of Raymond-Spartacus Kassoumi would satisfy the people's hunger for miraculous destinies and at the same time flatter the white man, who would squeal with glee that he had civilized his underdeveloped charge: *Ouhoum! gollè wari!*

There followed six months of bowing and scraping, of vituperation and treachery, of correspondence and council meetings at which the griots reviewed the political development of the sorrowful Nakem-Ziuko, threatened, so they sang, by Al Hadj Hassan—who, after having plotted against Saif with the help of Bishop Thomas de Saignac, was still trying, in his obstinate jealousy, to throw discredit on the mighty Saif and at the same time on Raymond, the most educated among the educated, as well.

Saif launched a vast campaign, culminating, two days before Raymond's arrival, in a civil war in Tillabéri-Bentia, which was rapidly quelled by France and Saif.

Al Hadj Hassan was imprisoned for crimes against the security of the colony. Unable, so it is said, to endure this taint on his rank, he cracked his skull against the walls of his cell. He was mourned by his servants, who, in confessing to Henry, their bishop, whispered that Saif had murdered him with the help of Kratonga, who had bribed the warden and the sentry—David Bouremi, Saif's adoptive son—and touched up the murder to look like suicide. . . .

Though exacerbated by this death and by tribal warfare, separatist sentiment was forgotten the following day when Raymond the builder was welcomed at the newly inaugurated airport by the governor, his high officials, Saif, yesterday's dissidents whom Madoubo had won over to Saif's side by appropriate gifts, and the people, delirious with enthusiasm.

How happy Tambira's son was to find himself acclaimed by all on the eve of the elections! With words of respect on their lips and affection in their eyes, old and young, clerks and dignitaries, made him presents—two sheep, three cows, twenty chickens, and thirty garments for his wife and son, and for himself a pair of red leather babouches embroidered with gold and silver.

That same morning Renard made a speech in Saif's honor, Raymond did likewise, and Saif replied; the people knelt, and in the midst of blaring bands, tanks, and salvoes of gunfire proclaiming his triumph the army honored him with a magnificent "Present arms": there was no other candidate.

Exhibited and loudly cheered from Tillabéri-Bentia to Krebbi-Katsena, where the governor had lodged him in his palace, he savored his consecration, his revenge on fate, with modesty. All that afternoon French and native personalities—an interminable parade—called to pay their respects and assure him of their devotion.

For Saif ben Isaac al-Heit, the task of subjecting the educated niggertrash was completed. But the master of Tillabéri-Bentia knew that it is easier to subjugate a people than to hold it down. And so, that very evening he sent a delegation of sages, elders, and marabouts to the cemetery to mourn Al Hadj Hassan, whose family received a royal gift of a thousand oxen.

Kassoumi the shrewd calculator had miscalculated: armed with his degrees and the support of France, he had expected to become his old master's master, when in reality the slave owed his election exclusively to the torch of Saif, more radiant than ever after a momentary lapse. *Yérété! aou yo yédè?*

Often, it is true, a man's heart rages and grieves when he sees his country juggling desperately with itself—an immense body in quest of its identity. That night of July 17, 1947, the seven hundred and forty-fifth anniversary of the founding of the Nakem Empire, Kassoumi thought sadly of the legend of the Saifs, a legend in which the future seems to seek itself in the night of time—prehistory in a tail coat: there stands the African.

Not that Raymond, at that inspired turning point in African civilization, embodied a mere intellectual protest. He knew that in spite of Saif his whole existence would be a protest: the condition of this country was scandalous beyond description.

But the notables here—as elsewhere the bourgeoisie—were prepared to turn this protest to their own use—labeling, wrapping, and selling even the sense of outrage. Vis-à-vis the traditionalists, Tambira's son, in the political role he aspired to play in the Nakem that had murdered his parents, remained a kind of artist, and like the artist in all societies he was free, because he himself was a problematic existence, a living conflict.

In this alienation, to be sure, Raymond-Spartacus Kassoumi

found an open door to revolt: for him and his Africa it was in a sense a duty to be revolutionary. But how . . . ?

His helpless bitterness was disarmed by the enthusiasm of Suzanne, flattered by the brilliant career that awaited them; and the builder realized to his horror that by his presence or by his death he would give publicity to Saif, who would take credit for anything he built.

Far from such thoughts, Suzanne's eyes lit up, shining with the cupidity of a venal woman; her husband hated her for loving him in this way, for worshiping his official personage; and burning with dull anger, he approached her.

Suzanne's mouth. Her lips are edged with honey-colored flesh. Her tongue, soft and light in her open mouth. He nibbles it, bites it, draws it to him, devours it, savoring his revenge. He zips open his trousers and presses the cavern of her lips to his long, rounded penis. Suzanne resists. Feebly. Tries to get up. But the prowling shuttle of his penis has fallen on her breasts. Immobile, passive, holding down the white woman's neck with both hands, he pours out his hatred. Her hair falls over her eyes as frantically, with trembling hands, she busies herself with his body and slips off his shorts. Set free, the ball of brown flesh dances and jogs. Like a fabulous fist it strikes her tongue, which licks the dark velvet of the two bulges at the base of the penis. Her clitoris—a smooth cleft swelling—is as hard as a date pit. She bends back, and presses his cudgel to her vulva, which caresses him, devours him, crushes him, and harvests his sap, laps it up, gathers it gently, takes the last gleanings. The long brown upright legs and wriggling contracting toes are the only witnesses to the serf's son's pleasure.

Springing to life, the woman comes back to surprise him with a long harvest of sticky delights, then she catches her breath and, conquered, slumps down on the floor.

His heart clothed in serenity, Raymond went to see Henry, who was about to set out for Tillabéri-Bentia—to see Saif.

"I'm going to be late," the bishop began, "and Saif is a stickler for form. . . . Let me come and see you tomorrow."

"Certainly," said Kassoumi.

In his voice there was a new intonation, a weariness and detachment that made the bishop prick up his ears.

"What's wrong, my friend?" he asked him with a look of perplexity.

"Nothing. Nothing at all."

Henry relaxed: "Sit down; would you care for a drink?"

"No, thank you. I'd rather walk along with you."

Holding his bicycle by the handlebars amid the crushing silence of the Nakem night, the bishop spoke as though he had just found an explanation for his old pupil's odd behavior.

"The Chinese have a game: the connecting link, they call it. They capture two birds and tie them together. Not too close. The cord is thin, strong, and fairly long. When the birds are released, they take flight, they think they are free and rejoice in the wideness of the sky. But suddenly: crack! The cord is stretched taut. They flutter and whirl in all directions, blood drips from their bruised wings, feathers and fluff fall on the onlookers. The Chinese find it subtly amusing, gloriously funny. They hold their sides with laughter. Sometimes the cord gets tangled in a branch or twines around the birds, and they struggle as though caught in a trap, peck at each other's eyes, beaks, and wings, and if Providence doesn't impale them on a branch, one of them dies before the game is over. Alone. Or with the other. Both of them. Together. Strangled; blinded.

"Mankind is such a bird. We are all victims of the game; separate, but tied together. All of us, without exception."

"But, but . . ." Raymond stammered.

"Yes?"

"You . . . Why are you telling me all this?"

"Because I have found out how Saif murders men with asps. And that concerns you. Come, let's be moving along.

"As you doubtless know, Saif is surrounded by sorcerers, excellent botanists who, preferably in the dry season, seek out clumps of reeds and ivy: those are the places where quails and partridges lay their eggs. And if they do, a snake is never far off.

What's the connection, you may ask. It's very simple. The snake feeds on the eggs.

"Very well. The sorcerer finds the snakes' nest. Those are harmless snakes. But going higher, among the rocks, if he is very patient, he can discover the hiding place of an asp. All he has to do is put a game bag at the entrance and smoke out the hole. The rest is only a question of strong nerves. With a quick movement he turns the game bag over, closes it, and laces it up, taking care to let the snake's tail stick out: a simple precaution. Otherwise it twists frantically in all directions and is likely to bite him when he opens the bag. Then he takes some *dabali*.

"This same *dabali*, you know, is used by the Zobos of the Yame for their miraculous fishing. They dam a branch of the river upstream and down, then they sprinkle the water with *dabali*. In the heat of the sun the drugged fish float, the fishermen need only bend down to pick them up by the hundreds. A good washing and they're fit to eat. But let's get back to our asps.

"The sorcerer fills the game bag half full of water and adds the *dabali*, which puts the asp to sleep. He waits a little while; when it's limp, he removes it from the bag.

"He takes its measurements: length and thickness. Then he hollows out a length of bamboo and puts the asp inside, leaving an inch or two of free space. He plugs up one end with a wooden stopper and the other with an undergarment stolen from the future victim.

"Remember, my friend, the very first crimes against the administration, committed around 1902, before the death of Chevalier. Yes, of course, that was before your time. But never mind: those crimes were committed with asps.

"Well, this undergarment should be as soiled as possible, impregnated with the smell of the victim. When the asp wakes up and tries to escape, the murderer removes the undergarment for a moment and puts it back again. Then he slips a needle through a hole in the cylinder. When the asp tries to get out, the murderer pricks its tail. The asp wriggles, hisses, butts its head against the undergarment and bites it. The operation is repeated until, super-

saturated and conditioned by the repetition close-prick-⟨
bite, the asp comes to identify the specific smell of the garment.

"You follow me? A time comes when there's no need to prick
the asp; the smell suffices to make it bite the garment, *a garment
with this particular smell, which it recognizes.*

"Steal a second garment from the victim; don't worry, I
haven't gone mad. Jean Barou the blacksmith told me all about
it before killing Doumbouya and being killed in turn. I myself,
on two occasions after the murder of Hassan, missed my . . ."

"It was a murder?"

"Definitely. And because I knew it, I came very close to being
killed. I don't have to tell you by whom. But let's not talk about
me.

"As I was saying, the murderer procures a second garment
belonging to the victim. And at night he drags it over the ground
to the 'troublemaker's' bed; then he goes back and opens the
cylinder—the snake comes out, crawls to the bed, bites, and dis-
appears. Where to? It takes the path traced by the murderer:
still guided by the smell of the undergarment, it comes back to
the murderer, who clubs it and puts it back in the game bag, or
else (and this is what was done in the case of the administrators
and missionaries) the snake is guided to an open space, where
there are people about, and a spy, in the criminal's pay, sets up a
shout of: 'Snake! Snake!' The rest is comedy. The snake is killed
in the presence of the stunned onlookers, who deplore the victim's carelessness. . . .

"And so, my poor Raymond, you have no choice. You've had
no choice since the day when you first sat down on a school
bench.

"I've told you this to put you on your guard. Don't forget
yourself in your dealings with Saif—for tomorrow you will be
elected. Remember this: in forty-five years of patient effort, I've
never been able to produce any evidence against him. That's
another story. It's getting late. I've got to be off to Tillabéri-
Bentia."

"To see Saif?"

"Yes."

"But that's suicide!" Raymond stammered.

"I'm going to see Machiavelli. Or Judas. Remember now: you're being elected tomorrow. That will be your day, my child. Good night."

**FOUR**

# Dawn

"Yesterday," said Bishop Henry after a while, "I went for a walk. Five minutes. A movie house. A picture, *Zamba,* inspired by the history of Nakem-Ziuko. I go in. The picture has started. I arrive in the middle of a massacre. A shot is fired. No. He's not dead: he's the hero.

"I don't understand. I try to piece the story together. On the one hand, I get a vague idea of the plot; on the other hand, carnage. Someone at the center of it all pulled the strings. When he pulled too hard, everyone could smell the melodramatic villain at work, and the audience grumbled. I look at the screen: anything goes—all the tortuous, silent, insidious, exalting, and fanatically religious methods of secret warfare. But for all those people the driving force is a self-testing, not so much to express a bloody vision of the world as to arrive at an immanent concordance between life and the world. The crux of the matter is that violence, vibrant in its unconditional submission to the will to power, becomes a prophetic illumination, a manner of questioning and answering, a dialogue, a tension, an oscillation, which from murder to murder makes the possibilities respond to each other, complete or contradict each other. The outcome is

...ertainty. But also a conflict between the rejection of decadence and nostalgia for a privileged experience, the forced quest of a morality provided with a false window offering a vista of happiness: the golden age when all the swine will die is just around the corner. All the characters are inhabited by fury. They show only the tips of their ears, they appear for an instant through a keyhole, and kill each other. And disappear. Frenzy vibrates on the screen, preserving our nostalgia for heroic periods and clandestinity. The clandestine plotter was a god, hunted and free; at every pistol shot he started off again from scratch, with a world of his choice, swine of his choice, pure hearts of his choice, and then, suddenly, bang!—freedom recaptured against a background of adventure and legend. . . ."

"Keep cool; if not, you'll be vulnerable," said Saif on a note of irony, suspecting the bishop of speaking in veiled words. "You mustn't imagine," he went on, clucking softly, "that the sun will never shine again. We are wanderers in disaster, that's a fact; but we fall, we are humble, we gargle with poison from the bloody cup of violence, the chipped glass of values; we are sick, degraded; but that's because the world *is* odd. Steeped in the strangest sediments ever churned by God in His chaotic blessing! I am quite capable of judging Him, and in so loud a voice that Satan would think he was listening to a jubilant angel nearby."

Then in a falsetto:

"You see, my friend, in Nakem we have a tale. Of men and their madness Destiny said: *'I must forgive them, mankind is so young.'* And it waited. And it's still waiting. Like patience on a monument. Isn't that delightful? But suddenly the unforeseen! The rules are thrown headlong: 'What broke down?' The whole human machine, the boiler was ready to burst and it burst. But Destiny is right there, and Destiny always forgives. Its pardon is signed by a cabinet minister: read and approved, place, date, and seal. That's what we call a reprieve; when it expires, mankind in its arch way starts all over again; and Destiny never wearies of forgiving, by proxy. How could it weary? If it did, would it not know Tedium, the empty consciousness of a time without content? The tedious innocence of one who has never sinned! But we are sinners. And God forgives. Out of constraint. Or out of love, perhaps."

"To the metal of many souls constraint is like a blow on flint: the spark that is struck is called love."

"Who cares for a love that is no more than a spark?"

"Man."

"You don't say. And why, my dear bishop?"

"Because life, once we live it, is faith in the love of life. . . . There are some who tell us that life is the aggregate of men's interests, and they add that to understand it we must live the experiences of other men. Perhaps; but I fail to understand a life of love that is not a priesthood, nor should I find it easy to understand a priest who was not an apostle."

"And so . . ."

"And so I thought of Nakem and its whole history. And I prayed."

"And what did you find out?"

"That God can be known but not understood."

"Is that so important?"

"Men kill each other because they have been unable to communicate."

"Yet they love each other, because when they separate it dawns on each one that he has spoken only of himself. Have you never missed your target, failed to reach those you love?"

"Yes, for years: because I tried to act on others instead of letting them find themselves. . . ."

"You were speaking of Nakem just now."

"I wanted to be alone and pure."

"But solitude goes hand in hand with a feeling of guilt, of complicity. . . ."

"I beg your pardon," the bishop countered. "Of solidarity."

"Man is in history, and history is in politics. Politics is cleavage. No solidarity is possible. Nor purity."

"The essential is to despair of purity and to believe one is right to despair. Love is nothing else. Politics does not know the goal but forges a pretext of a goal. Regimes collapse because their politicians don't know how to handle the forge."

"But their awkwardness is unavoidable, because politics is seldom honestly expressed, or rather, politics does not lend itself to honest expression."

The bishop laughed heartily.

"That is quite true," he conceded, "though I seem to detect a note of sarcasm. . . . You see" (he rested his elbows on the table, crossed his fingers, and looked at Saif with an indulgent smile, a smile of complicity), "that is why I have been able to understand Nakem and its history." Saif felt uncomfortable, vaguely ill at ease, but still the bishop smiled gently. Then shrugging his shoulders, Henry asked nonchalantly: "Have you some game we could play? Chess?"

After a brief hesitation Saif turned to Henry with a strange look. He was visibly disappointed.

"I thought you understood me," he said. "I was sure."

Henry's glance was firm and penetrating, and again Saif experienced a feeling of terror and vague complicity.

"Anyway, it doesn't matter; am I right?"

"Absolutely."

"How long have you had that conviction?"

The bishop stopped to think. "I believe I was born with it," he said. "To know, as you and I know, that we are bent on the impossible, is probably a form of love or madness. Yet, it comes from our faculty, or need, of attaching ourselves to reality."

"Yes. . . ."

A silence followed. Saif rubbed his lips to conceal a smile, then rose to get the chessmen. At the same time he brought back a bamboo cylinder which he put down on the floor. As though wishing to justify himself:

"I warn you. I don't know how to play."

"Exactly."

"What do you mean?"

"It's quite simple. You play the game. But you don't let yourself be made game of.

"But keep your eye on the other man's play," Henry insisted, still with the same smile of connivance. "You must learn to know it and to know yourself in it. Say to yourself," he continued with calculated ambiguity: *"I want to play as if they did not see me playing,* entering into my game without ostentation, appearing to be in accord with myself and with them, making use of their guile without ever seeming to face it head on or trying to divert it, exposing the intricate trap, but with caution, never touching anything until I have fathomed its hidden mechanism. Without such caution, my friend, can you hope to kill your adversary . . . in a game?"

Saif understood; he knew that Henry knew. But the bishop went on imperturbably:

"So you see, that man is a good player who is able to hide his game and abide by his plan." And suddenly, raising his eyebrows with an air of polite surprise: "The very essence of the game of diplomacy is to *replace force with ruse*. . . ."

Draping himself in all the splendor of his personage, Saif: "You know, my friend, you don't solve a problem of civilization; you devote yourself to it, and first of all you let yourself be guided by it. The law of justice and love is the only bond that is capable of uniting our irreducible diversities—from above. Down below, amid the strange fauna of the human passions, the lust for power and glory is at work. But that's where you and I complement each other. There lies our wealth and true kinship."

The cylinder began to move very slowly and waveringly toward Henry, who read in Saif's eyes that in that moment he was exposing both their lives to the faint hisses that issued from it. Both pretended to be aware of nothing, and yet the looks in their eyes established a strange bond between them.

"But you know," Saif laughed, "I'm incapable of guile."

"You're making a big mistake," said Henry with a smile. "Man . . . uh . . . is a political animal, don't you agree? In other words, guile is the essence of power and justice, the art of dialoguing with life."

"Man *is* evil," said Saif slowly.

Both burst out laughing.

"You're making a big mistake in spurning guile," the bishop repeated.

The old man's eyes were bright and serene. A detached smile hovered on his lips. As their eyes met, Saif had the impression that this man shared his secret, that they were the only authentic conspirators in Nakem-Ziuko. Both had faced up to the ultimate lie or the ultimate truth of existence.

"Guile?" Saif expressed his astonishment cautiously, almost fearfully, as though sensing a mysterious, supernatural power in his interlocutor's quiet smile. He looked at the bishop with an expression of mingled affection and fear.

"Guile is freedom," Henry replied. "The idea of freedom is not a simple one. It is forever changing. Just like the structure of a game. One and the same idea has many moments. Taken at a given moment of its movement, an idea should reveal itself in the substance of its definition. Men believe they are free the moment the law is recognized and stated. Play. I'll tell you the rules. You will exist."

"*Amen.* Existence can conform to the law but cannot be deduced from it. Play! We are responsible for the success of the stratagem."

Both waited to see who would begin. And the bishop, awkward but respectful:

"If you can't make up your mind, it means that you don't want to know what you secretly desire and refuse to take cognizance of what you are."

(The cylinder quivered and rolled between them.) "One must learn the art," said Henry, "of making mistakes intelligently and covering up one's tracks."

"Why?" Saif smiled. There was a certain complacency in the graceful curve of his lips.

"Just look: the squares, the pawns lined up like soldiers in the night of Nakem, the two fools,* Chevalier and Vandame, the two knights, Kratonga and Wampoulo, the two rooks, Kassoumi and Bouremi. Look! The queen. The most powerful of all: she

* French *fou* = fool and, in chess, bishop.

moves in all directions, the others have only one direction. And all that, the whole panoply, is only to save the king's head—your conscience—the immobilized piece. You see? All that! . . . to defend the king. You face life in a brotherly confrontation of your forces, and you play, you calculate, you play, you adapt, you fall, yes, no, watch out, every move counts, you calculate . . .

"God or Devil—and you right your boat again. And you live. And you transcend life."

Saif's eyes threw sparks. The cylinder swayed from Henry to Saif, from Ṣaif to Henry, who said in a tone of mockery:

"Ought I to be afraid?"

"Afraid? Of whom? Of what? Of yourself? Of me? Of us, of *that*? I warn you . . . you mustn't be afraid!"

"Or else?" asked the bishop, taking up the challenge.

"Or you'll curse yourself for having underestimated your strength. And anyway, what does it matter? Play! Each player is a functional object, a plaything and at the same time the stake of the game. Try to trap your opponent."

"And if he holds back?"

"From what?"

"From making his move."

"He doesn't hold back; he won't hold back. He's an opponent. You've got to catch him in that aggressive, pendular movement in which one tension arouses another; each player aims to destroy the other's trap."

"But what if it's meaningless, absurd?"

"Absurd isn't the same as meaningless. Nature has no meaning, but it's not absurd. It *is*. The absurd springs from things that destroy and engender one another. It is this concept of the absurd that underlies unjustifiable acts."

At once flattered and embarrassed by this homage to his intelligence, the bishop cried: "The cylinder is dancing. It's rolling toward me. Kill, Saif"—so revealing that he knew there was an asp hidden in the cylinder.

Suddenly Saif's face erupted. The shock—as the bishop could sense—released a succession of regular, almost rhythmic tremors. It wasn't fear—of that Henry was well aware—or remorse, but excitement in anticipation of what was to come. Saif rubbed his jaw thoughtfully.

"I haven't the right," he said, surveying the bishop with the heavy anguish of his gray eyes.

HENRY: "You mean, you haven't the might," he replied gently.

SAIF: "No, I haven't the right," he insisted.

HENRY: "Right without might is a caricature. Might without right is abomination. Admit it."

SAIF: "There's nothing to admit. The triumph of right is the triumph of its might. And besides . . . your game . . ."

HENRY: *"The* game."

SAIF: ". . . The game and all that, it's too exhausting." (And a moment later, as though smitten with grace:) "The adversary," he confessed, "is so constituted that we always think him the cleverer. There is no way out."

HENRY: "The moment we came into the world, we were caught up in the game. We've got to take chances. Go ahead. Kill!" the bishop insisted.

(Saif looked at the cylinder as though it had come into his hands by magic.)

SAIF: "Do you want me to kill you?" he asked Henry with an air of bewilderment.

HENRY: "Why not?" (And as the bishop looked on with an amused smile, Saif suddenly, without a word, took the cylinder, threw it into the fire, and came back to Henry.)

SAIF: "You see, there's too much coercion."

HENRY: "Of course," he smiled. "It's a game." (And he added in a changed voice:) *"A game that has its rules."*

SAIF: "Then there's no choice."

HENRY: "Oh yes there is. You become free because you have no choice."

(The two men exchanged smiles and for the first time agreed to speak the same language.)

SAIF: "Symbols never die," he said, as the asp he had trained crackled in the fire. "Nakem was born generations ago, and only in the last fifteen minutes have men learned to discuss the state of its health."

HENRY: "But the king will not die."

SAIF: "Play! Queen."

HENRY: "In any case, where love is concerned . . . Knight."

SAIF: "There is always one who loves and the other who turns his cheek. Pawn."

HENRY: "One must know how to live. Play! King."

SAIF: "The impossible part of forgiveness is that one must keep it up. Play! Queen."

HENRY: "Life is no different. Play! Blessed are the peace-makers. For they shall see God. Praised be."

SAIF: "Play! Blessed are the politicians, for they shall understand life. The Eternal One."

HENRY: "Play! And may the troubadours in Nakem sing the history of Judaism. King."

SAIF: "And praised be. Play! Saif Moshe Gabbai of Honain. Queen."

HENRY: "The Eternal One. Play! Saif Isaac al-Heit."

SAIF: "Amen. Play! Saif al-Hilal."

HENRY: "May the Nakem of the empires be in our souls. Play! Saif al-Haram. King."

SAIF: "And praised be. Play! Saif Ali. Queen."

HENRY: "The Eternal One. Play! Saif Yussufi. Fool."

SAIF: *"Yallah al'allah!* Play! Saif Medioni of Mostaganem. Rook."

HENRY: "So be it. Play! Saif Ezekiel. Pawn."

SAIF: "And praised be. Play! Saif Ismail. Knight."

HENRY: "The Eternal One. Play! Saif Benghighi of Saida."

SAIF: "Amen. Play! Saif Rabban Johanan ben Zakkai."

HENRY: "So be it. Play! Saif Tsevi. King."

SAIF: *"Mashallah! wa bismillah!* Play! Saif ben Isaac al-Heit. Queen."

Often, it is true, the soul desires to dream the echo of happiness, an echo that has no past. But projected into the world, one cannot help recalling that Saif, mourned three million times, is forever reborn to history beneath the hot ashes of more than thirty African republics.

. . . That night, as they sought one another until the terrace was soiled with the black summits of dawn, a dust fell on the chessboard; but in that hour when the eyes of Nakem take flight in search of memories, forest and coast were fertile and hot with compassion. And such was the earth of men that the balance between air, water, and fire was no more than a game.

## Selected titles from the African Writers Series

**The Last of the Empire**

*Sembene Ousmane*

Translated from the French by Adrian Adams

Senegal's President, Leon Mignane, has mysteriously vanished. His Cabinet splits into rival factions as popular unrest grows—until the Army steps in. The elderly Minister of Justice comes to see himself as the survivor of an era of corruption and compromise that the young now rightly reject as "the last of the Empire".

1983   256pp   0 435 90250 4   AWS 250

**The Poor Christ of Bomba**

*Mongo Beti*

Translated from the French by Gerald Moore

In Bomba the girls who are being prepared for Christian marriage live together in the women's camp. Gradually it becomes apparent that the local churchmen have been using the local girls for their own purposes.

1971   224pp   0 435 90088 9   AWS 88

**Houseboy**

*Ferdinand Oyono*

Translated from the French by John Reed

Written in the form of a diary kept by a Camerounian houseboy, it tells of his fascination with the world of his white masters.

"It is a better guide to French Colonial Africa, and to racism, than any non-fiction account, whether by African or Frenchman."

*The Times Literary Supplement*

1966   144pp   0 435 90029 3   AWS 29

*Continued overleaf*

**Two Thousand Seasons**

*Ayi Kwei Armah*

A young group inexorably rebels against the forces destroying Africa. In a universe poisoned with the deadly values of the West, how shall a people devoted to life prevail?

"It stays in the mind as sermon, as lush imagery, but chiefly as a story of change, through cruelty suffered and inflicted, to the abiding beauty of the creative purpose of our relationships."

*Tribune*

1979   224pp   0 435 90218 0   AWS 218